Living on Seashell Isla
By
Brenda Kennedy

Dedicated to Mom, who loved my dad with her entire heart and being.

LULU EDITION

LULU ISBN: 978-1-387-64105-5

This is a work of fiction. Names, characters, businesses, places, events, and incidents are either the products of the author's imagination or used in a fictitious manner. Any resemblance to actual persons, living or dead, or actual events is purely coincidental.

All rights reserved. No parts of this publication may be reproduced, distributed, or transmitted in any form or by any means, including photocopying, recording, or other electronic or mechanical methods, without the prior written permission of the author, except in the case of brief quotations embodied in critical reviews and certain noncommercial uses permitted by the author. For permission requests, email the author at brendakennedy48@gmail.com.

Synopsis

After mourning her deceased husband for more than two decades, Grace Stewart feels like she's able to finally move on. With the assistance of her family, she opens a candle and craft shop on Seashell Island, and with their continued support she slowly starts to rebuild her life.

Taking it one day at a time, Grace begins to enjoy and appreciate her independence and her decision to live again. She realizes she didn't die the dreadful night her husband, Michael, did, although she did stop living so many years ago.

Grace is surprised and excited when Doctor James Taylor shows an interest in her and asks her out. Grace finds herself with feelings she never expected to have again. James is everything she's ever dreamed of.

But when someone accuses James of misconduct, Grace begins to question if he's really the man she thought he was. Does love continue to blossom on Seashell Island, or does Grace find herself heartbroken and alone?

TABLE OF CONTENTS

CAST OF CHARACTERS	1
PROLOGUE	2
CHAPTER 1	3
CHAPTER 2	30
CHAPTER 3	52
CHAPTER 4	73
CHAPTER 5	96
CHAPTER 6	107
CHAPTER 7	126
CHAPTER 8	142
CHAPTER 9	161
BOOKS BY BRENDA KENNEDY	182
ACKNOWLEDGEMENTS	184
ABOUT THE AUTHOR	187

CAST OF CHARACTERS

James Taylor: Main character and Parker's father

Grace Stewart: Main character and Sarah and Carly's mother

Sarah Stewart: Grace's daughter

Parker Blake: Sarah's boyfriend and the island's MD

Carly Stewart Romano: Grace's daughter

Beau Romano: Carly's husband

Myra: Beau's daughter from a previous marriage

Baby Maria: Beau and Carly's daughter

Tony: Beau's father

Larry, aka Pap: Grace's Dad and Sarah and Carly's grandfather

Sylvia aka Gram: Grace's Mom and Sarah and Carly's grandmother

Julie: James' office manager

Matt: An ex-employee

Anna: Nurse

PROLOGUE

When my husband died over two decades ago, I died right along with him. I had just turned thirty and was happily married to the love of my life, raising two very young beautiful daughters, and running a successful candle and craft business. My life was right where I wanted it.

Then I got the call that changed my life forever. The news that the love of my entire life, the father of our beautiful daughters, was killed in a head-on car accident.

I was left sad and alone. Unable to make simple decisions and at the insistence of my mother and father, I sold my business and our home, and then my daughters and I moved in with them.

On the day my husband died, twenty-two years ago, I died right along with my soulmate.

CHAPTER 1

GRACE

I wake up to birds chirping outside my bedroom window. The salty ocean air fills my nostrils as it breezes in from the ocean. Nothing says a new beginning like the first day of spring. That's the sole reason why I chose today, the first day of spring, to start living again.

My daughter Sarah wrote this haiku, which is apt:

SUDDENLY

***

cold, dreary, dismal

winter, snow, depression, and

then cherry blossoms

On Christmas Eve my mom and dad bought the only floral shop on Seashell Island and gifted it to me. They decided that it was time for me to move on with my life. Sadly, I knew it was true. Mourning my dead husband for twenty-two years was long enough. Too long.

For the last three months, I've worked on trying to move on. I know it's time. There's no set limit on the amount of time you should mourn the loss of someone. Michael was my life; he was my everything. How do you put a time frame on your sadness?

But every day since Christmas, I've worked on myself and having a project to focus my attention on was a huge help in finding myself again. The floral shop and the small two-bedroom apartment over it were already in great condition, but it wasn't me or my style. I wanted light and bright colors with a mixture of shabby chic, farmhouse style, and coastal décor. I wanted a place that was casual and inviting.

Open and airy. I wanted someplace that visitors would visit and want to come back to. The same goes for my home. I wanted a home where guests would feel welcome. I also wanted my home to feel like a retreat for me. Something relaxing and comforting.

I have to admit, it wasn't easy in the beginning. I felt guilty for living. I felt guilty for breathing and having a life with Michael gone. But slowly and one step and one day at a time I could feel myself healing and it felt good.

With everything freshly painted and decorated, I spent the first night in twenty-two years in my own place. Alone. I had company late into the evening and once my parents, kids, and grandkids left, they all decided to call and check up on me.

This morning, I have my coffee while sitting on the balcony before my shower. My mind immediately drifts to my life with Michael… well, before his death. Sadness begins to set in until I shift my thinking to the here and now. Feeling rejuvenated, I stand and welcome the first day of spring into my life.

Before I open the store at ten o'clock, my daughters, Carly and Sarah, and my parents show up to help me with any last-minute adjustments I may have. While Sarah lights a few scattered candles inside, Dad and I carry the white steel bench outside and set it under the large picture window. Carly brings out and sets up a display of wreaths and a few floral arrangements for the onlookers to see. Mom props open the front door in hopes the scent from the vanilla candles will lure locals and the tourists into the shop. I stand and look at the old floral shop and I'm proud of the new updates.

Sarah's boyfriend, Parker, and Carly's husband, Beau, also come for the grand opening. In all honesty, the more people who are here, the more my anxiety builds. But I'm excited to see what this next chapter of my life will bring me. I know Michael is smiling down on me and watching over his family.

This reminds me of when I opened my first shop when the girls were little. Grand openings weren't big back then, but Michael surprised me with a celebration party and a cake in the shape of my new candle shop, complete with the shop's name. Michael was proud of me. A single tear slides down my cheek at the memory.

I didn't want to, but Carly and Sarah both insisted on doing a name reveal for my shop. I didn't keep the previous name since it's no longer a floral shop. As the streets come alive with tourists and locals browsing the local shops, Dad and Beau replace the white and black sign over the store with one that was more nautical. A white sign with navy blue scripted letters hangs above the door. I decided to keep the same name I had before when I ran my own business: "Grace's Candles, Wreaths, and Crafts."

A photographer from the small island newspaper is also here taking photos and interviewing me on my new business adventure. Once the sign's been revealed, the crowd starts gathering inside the shop.

"Congratulations, Grace," Parker says as he kisses me on my cheek. "I'd love to stay, but I have a medical practice to run."

"I understand. Thanks for stopping by."

"I'm glad to be able to share in your big day," he adds.

"Me, too, Mom," Sarah says. "Everything looks amazing."

I look adoringly at Sarah. "Thank you."

"I'll stop over on my lunch break and see if you need help with anything."

"She'll be fine, Sarah. I'll be here if she needs anything," Mom says, following a customer into the shop.

"Sarah, your grandmother's right. I have plenty of help. You and Parker should just focus on healing the ill and treating the injured."

"While Parker's the one who saves lives, I'll be the one pulling patient medical charts and collecting co-pays." Sarah loops her arm through Parker's. "I'm just there for the paycheck." She laughs as they walk away.

Carly walks up to me and asks, "She's just kidding, right?"

"We can only hope."

"I have to go, too." Carly gives me a tight hug. "I am so proud of you."

"Thank you."

"Mom, I'll be right up the street if you need me."

"I'll be fine, Carly. Have a great day and sell lots of books." I smile and watch as my daughter walks to her own shop.

"I have to go to the market so Dad can come over here and wish you well. He told me not to be gone long," Beau says.

I hug Beau. "Thank you for coming. It wouldn't be the same without Tony here. Kiss my grandchildren for me, will you?"

"You know it. If you're slow later, maybe we'll stop by and see how it's going."

"I would like that." I look around at the spectators. Hopefully they're more than just watching; hopefully they'll be paying customers, too.

As my family leaves, more customers walk into the store. Dad and I decide we should go in and help Mom. I figured most of the customers today would be locals checking out the store and comparing it to the flower shop so they can see the changes I made. Most people don't like change so I expected some negative comments throughout the day. To my surprise, they seem happy to have a variety of items available. But I'm not surprised at how fast my dye-free, scented soy wax candles and wax melts sell.

Some of the candles I'm selling are made by a Jewish candle-maker whose grandmother was in Auschwitz. Her grandmother made candles for the Shabbat each week out of margarine she saved and a few strings she pulled from the bottom of her dress. Other women at Auschwitz did the same thing, and so each Friday they were able to light a few candles to celebrate Shabbat. According to her grandmother, those candles were the only reason she survived Auschwitz. Of course, the candles I sell in the shop are made with better materials, but I am sure that the Shabbat candles in Auschwitz burned more brightly.

Although I've just recently started making candles again, one thing I know a lot about are candles, fragrance oil, wick types, and wax. My candles are just as good as any name brand out there.

When I hear a powerful male voice, I look up and see Beau's father, Tony, walking into the shop. "Look at you," he says.

Tony and I have known each other since we were in our twenties. Tony lost his wife, Maria, to cancer a few years ago and like me, has remained single.

I walk into his open arms for a hug. "Thank you for coming."

"I wanted to come sooner but the market's been busy." He looks around the shop. "Ah, Maria would like this place."

"Thank you, Tony."

He laughs at a memory. "If she was still here, I'd have to get another job just to pay for her candle addiction."

She did like her candles. "I miss her," I admit.

"Me, too. Every day."

He walks around the shop and browses the different display areas while I attend to yet another customer. And to my surprise, they aren't all locals. Many are tourists who are here on vacation. Mom and Dad chat with everyone who enters the shop. Thankfully, they aren't pushing the merchandise as much as they're just having a leisurely chat with people. I'm definitely more of an introvert.

Tony makes a purchase of two candles before he leaves.

Today brought many emotions. Hour by hour I begin to feel whole. Like I can do this. Like this is what I was meant to do. I feel Michael in my heart and although he's gone, he's still very much alive inside me and I think he would be happy for me. Maybe even proud of me.

"Mom and Dad, you both can go. I think Carly and Beau could use your help with the girls."

"What if you get a rush?" Dad asks.

"Thank you, Dad. I'll be fine. Really." I know these words are difficult to believe, especially coming from me, their daughter who's lived with them the past twenty-two years because I couldn't come to terms with my husband's demise. I smile so they can see for themselves that the words are true. "I'll call if I need help."

Mom smiles, then nods. "Okay, we'll be back at closing time."

"Sounds perfect."

Although I'm grateful for their help, I could use some time alone to take it all in. A light breeze blows into the store and I inhale the scent of a vanilla candle. Is there anything better than that? Not today there isn't.

I watch as they slowly walk out of the store and head in the direction of Carly's bookstore. I'm grateful for the times that I'm busy and also for the down time. While walking through the store, I'm happy to see that everything is arranged nicely.

As I cash out a woman who bought one of the romance books Carly's written, I tell her, "The author of the book also owns the bookstore a few doors down. I know for a fact that she'll be happy to autograph the book for you." I don't tell her the author is my daughter, although it's hard not to boast about that.

"Oh, a local author. A double bonus. In that case, I'll buy another one for my sister: Mildred. Mildred just loves books. You know, this kind," she says, fanning the pages of the book in my direction. "She could never get used to reading a book on one of those electronic devices. I'm with Mildred. I also need pages to turn. It just doesn't seem right having a book stored in some cyber cloud or whatever it is they call it."

"Thank you and I hope you come back." She and her sister do have a point; I also like a paperback book to hold. And yet I realize that people who read a book a day are likely to prefer eBooks. Fortunately, this world has room for both kinds of books. I watch as she makes her way out of the store in the direction of Carly's bookstore. I also tossed in a couple of postcards featuring Sarah's haiku poems. They are for sale but are free with a purchase of a book.

One of the postcards shows two little girls holding hands and running — one little girl just ahead of the other — across the field. This is the haiku:

Come with me because

Over there's an adventure

I can see it now

The other postcard shows my store. This is the haiku:

Exploring bookshelves

Prospecting for golden words

Such an adventure

If Sarah wasn't working at her fiancé's medical practice and shouldn't be disturbed, I would have also sent my customer to her to get the postcards autographed. It's hard to keep from bragging about my children.

Sarah comes over at lunch and brings us both salads and water she bought from Tony's market. We have a working lunch since I see no reason to close. It feels great being able to eat and visit with her. I've forgotten what it feels like to be normal. To feel like you fit in. This is what it feels like to live, to be alive. All those years wasted. All those years I mourned for my soulmate. It still makes me sad thinking about Michael so I quickly focus on something else. He would want me to move on. He'd be upset with me to know that after his death I nearly gave up on my own life. If it weren't for Carly and Sarah, I would have given up completely.

"How's work going for you?" I ask my beautiful daughter.

"It's good. Parker's busy."

"I bet he is. He's the only doctor on the entire island."

"I guess I never really thought about it before I started working there."

I watch as she takes a bite of her salad. "Have you two set a wedding date yet?"

"We've been kicking around some ideas."

"Valentine's Day of next year?" I ask.

"What about April Fool's Day?"

"Are you serious?" This is definitely a Sarah thing to do. To get married on the least likely day. She takes after her father. Michael proposed to me on Halloween. It took me a long time to realize he was serious because he was dressed as a vampire. We were getting ready to leave for a costume party.

"We're not sure. It's just a thought."

"You are serious?" I'm not sure why I even asked as I know she is. But then again, I'm hoping she's kidding. But why should I care. It's her wedding. Let them get married on any day they want.

"Parker thought about Valentine's Day, but I wanted a day that isn't over saturated with weddings and anniversaries. I wanted my own special day." She laughs as she thinks about all the millions of people who get married and she realizes there's no way for her to have "her own" day. But then again, how many Sarahs are there in the world who have chosen April Fool's Day as a day to become husband and wife?

I look lovingly at my daughter, and she deserves her own day. I like Parker and although their relationship blossomed quickly, it's easy to see he's a good match for my Sarah. I knew she had commitment issues, but I didn't know he did also. Short courtship… long engagement. That's my Sarah. Always doing things backwards.

"Do you have any other plans made for the wedding?" I ask.

"No, not yet, but do you think Pap would let us marry in the church?"

Sadness hits me with a rush. Why would she think her grandfather wouldn't allow her to marry in the church? "Yes, I'm sure he would let you." I reach over and take her hand. "Why on earth would you think otherwise?"

"Well, you know." Her eyes glisten with unshed tears. "I haven't always made the right choices in my life and I know I've let you, Gram, and Pap down."

I can't think of one time when either of my children disappointed me. Ever. "Sarah, look at me." I wait until she lifts her head so she can see me. "You have never done anything that would have made us ashamed of you. Ever. Not once."

Tears fall from her eyes. "Really?"

"Yes. Really. Some of the 'wrong' decisions you made brought you a lot of fun and it may have brought you some pain. Your father always said that he never regretted any kind of fun, even if other people regarded it as sinful. And your Pap would be thrilled for you to marry in the church."

"Good. That makes me feel better."

"Stop thinking that we could ever be disappointed in you for anything. We love you and we are so incredibly proud of you and your sister."

"Thank you, Mom."

"I think we're going to ask him this weekend." She takes a sip of her water.

Some customers walk in and I stand to greet them. "Back to work. I love you and I'll see you later."

Sarah picks up the trash and takes it with her. I wave goodbye before greeting the customer.

Throughout the day, I receive cards and flowers from a few of the locals wishing me well on my new business. But the last delivery is one that threw me off guard. Inside the box were several jars of homemade jams and jellies from a shop in Charlotte. I love homemade jams but not everyone knows that about me. The return address is from James Taylor. I don't know a James Taylor, other than the famous singer who sang "Fire and Rain," whom I've only heard about. The only other James I know is Parker's dad and Parker's last name's Blake. After reading the attached card, I learn that it is from Parker's father.

This delivery surprised me on so many levels. I've met the man only once and it was at our family Christmas Eve party. James drew my name for the gift exchange, and although the gifts weren't personal, they were nice and thoughtful. We chatted a few times and exchanged glances throughout the night. I smile as I read the labels of each of the decorative glass jars. This is very thoughtful. I have to wonder why Parker's dad would have gone through so much trouble to buy and send these when a card would have sufficed. He didn't have to do either; it wasn't necessary. Of course, he could have ordered them online, but it has a personal card attached with his signature.

Maybe he did it since we'll be a combined family. My daughter is marrying his son. I also remember how much I enjoyed his company.

***

Later that night, I have a glass of wine and take a bubble bath. I reflect solely on the day. I don't think about Michael or dwell on his death. Today is about me and living. The shop had a very productive first day. I had lunch with my daughter Sarah alone for the first time in I can't remember when.

After my shower, I dress in sweatpants and a hoodie and have another glass of wine outside on the balcony. I watch as the shops and street vendors close up for the night. A man in dark clothes looks up at me and waves. It's not quite dark, but it's too dark for me to tell who it is.

"How are you, Grace?"

I smile and focus my attention on him. I can't tell who it is. I decide it must be a customer. "I'm fine, how are you?"

"I'm good."

I think I recognize the voice. "James?" He looks up and smiles. "Are you looking for Parker and Sarah?"

"Right now, I'm looking for a place to get a coffee."

I laugh as most of the island is closing down for the night. If he wants beer or wine, he could go to the Jo's Tiki Hut. There's also a few restaurants still open for dinner. I decide to extend an invitation.

"Well, you're in luck. Café Grace is still opened."

I see hope in his eyes. "Are you serious? You're offering me coffee?"

I stand from my seat and offer a kind smile. "I'll be down in a second to let you in."

"Thank you," he says, walking toward my shop.

I rinse out my wine glass and place it in the dishwasher before heading downstairs to let James in. When I open the door, I'm greeted with a handsome smile. He looks a lot like Parker. He's tall and lean with a square jawline. His hair is dark although graying at the temples. He has kind eyes and a friendly smile. No wrinkles around his eyes and mouth except for some laugh lines and I wonder if it's good genes or Botox. His face is expressive, so it must be good genes. The way he's smiling, it seems like he was born with the happy gene.

"Are you lost or something?" I tease.

"It would appear so." He walks in and brings a light breeze with him. He's wearing Levi's and a navy-blue hoodie. I've seen him only a couple other times, and he was dressed in a suit and tie at our Christmas Eve party and then the next day at church. I have to admit that this casual look certainly looks good on him. He also smells good. Like spice, sandalwood, and musk. He says, "I'm here visiting for a few days, but I wanted to give Sarah and Parker some privacy."

"So you left in search of some coffee."

"Exactly."

Closing the door behind him, I motion toward the stairs. "Follow me." When we walk past the counter with the homemade jellies and jams, I stop. "You sent me these today?" I ask, not really knowing if it was him or not.

"I'm glad they arrived safely."

"Thank you, but why and how could you have known that I loved these?"

"Call it a house-warming gift, if you will. Parker told me when I had your name for the Christmas gift exchange. He wanted to make sure you received a decent gift."

Walking to the coffee pot, I say, "I remember the gifts you got me for the gift exchange and I thought they were all very nice."

"Thank you. Since I didn't get you any homemade jams, I thought this was a good reason to send them."

"You didn't have to send anything."

"It's not a big deal. It's not every day someone moves into their own place and opens up their own business." While I add water into the water reservoir for the coffee, he asks, "How was your first day?"

I look up at him. "It was a good day. A bit exhausting, but overall everything went very well."

He looks at his watch for the time. "If you're too tired, I can leave. I didn't mean to interrupt."

"No. I'm sorry. That's not what I was implying. I just meant being on your feet and running a business was tiring. I forgot how great it felt to be doing something productive."

"Sarah told me you were a stay-at-home mom while she was growing up."

I add the coffee and push the start button on the coffee maker. I never felt the need to explain myself or the events that led up to my decision to stay home with my girls. Not that I dread one moment of the time I spent at home with them, I just know now how unhealthy it was for me to have been so closed off from the world after Michael's death.

"I was. Their father passed away when they were very young so I sold my business, similar to the one I have now, and devoted my time to Sarah and Carly." I was very depressed but I don't say that.

"I'm sorry to hear of your loss. I wasn't aware of their father's passing."

"Thank you. It's no secret and it's been a long time ago."

"Parker's mother also passed away."

I look into his dark eyes that are filled with sadness, maybe regret and guilt. "No. I never knew that." My mind replays what I do know about Parker and James and I realize how little I do know about either of them. "I'm sorry for your and his loss."

"Thank you. Although it's been some time ago, some days it's still hard to believe."

I get that. "Time moves on, but some days it feels like it just stays dormant."

"Exactly." We both remain quiet as we listen to the coffee brew. "So, this is your new place," he says, looking around the small two-bedroom, two-bath apartment.

I look around proudly at my new home. "It is, let me give you the grand tour." While stepping out of the kitchen into the middle of the open floor plan living room, I point with my finger. Living room, dining room or breakfast nook, bedroom with its own bathroom, a guest bathroom, guest bedroom, kitchen, and balcony."

We both laugh at how small my place is. He was given the grand tour without taking a step into any of the rooms. At least it's not so small that I can touch door handles from the center of the living room. I remember that comedian Fred Allen joked that he once stayed in a hotel room that was so small the mice were hunchbacked.

"Very nice."

"Thank you. You can look around if you want. There isn't much to see."

He walks over to my bedroom and peeks his head into the door. "It's very warm and cozy and did I mention the wonderful aroma. It smells like you're baking cookies or something."

Warm and cozy is exactly the look and feel I was going for. I inhale deeply. "Candles. It's vanilla-scented candles that you're smelling."

"I'll need to come back during normal business hours. I'm often told my place smells of disinfectant or antibacterial spray."

I wonder if the person who told him that was his girlfriend. "I have some candles I can send with you tonight, or if you want a better selection we can go down to the shop."

"I'm in no hurry. I'll come back tomorrow when I can actually look around."

Walking back into the kitchen to check on the coffee, I ask, "How long are you staying?"

"I'm due back to work on Monday."

"You'll be here for the weekend. They're having a Spring Fling down on the beach this weekend. You should definitely go."

"Spring Fling?" He laughs.

While pouring the coffee into two mugs, I also laugh at the name. "It's a party they do annually to draw in tourists and locals as a way to welcome spring."

"After the bitter winter, spring is a welcome sight."

"It was bitter and spring is very welcome. The craft vendors will be busy selling their handmade products, and food vendors will also be lining the beaches and the streets selling food and beverages. They also have boat races, fishing tournaments, and games for the kids to compete in."

"Sounds like a must see."

"It is. I think it'll be something you might enjoy." I smile at a thought. "And if you don't, you'll know not to attend it next year." He laughs at my comment. "Would you like cream or sugar for your coffee?" I ask.

"Black, please." I hand him his mug and I lift mine to my mouth and inhale the delicious aroma before taking a sip. "Do you want to walk down by the water with our coffee?"

"Sure, I'd love to. Let me change first."

JAMES

When I met Grace at her family's Christmas Eve party, I knew she wouldn't be one I could forget easily. I knew nothing about her except that she was Sarah's mother. Her family welcomed me into their home without ever meeting me. This family is a rare find in these times of mistrust and violence.

I met Sarah briefly and liked her immediately. She was sweet, beautiful, and very intelligent. I liked everything about her. What wasn't there to like? I knew just from looking at my son that he was also smitten by her. I also knew she was an amazing girl, but I didn't know how amazing until I met her family.

As I wait for Grace, I remain standing at the door as I scan her quaint apartment. The apartment is decorated in nautical décor. I don't know her well enough to know what her style is. I'm not sure if she decorated it or if the apartment came furnished and decorated. Maybe she hired an interior designer.

She smiles as she makes her way out of the bedroom, wearing a pale pink color sweatshirt, jeans, and tennis shoes. Her blond hair is shoulder length and straight. I can tell by the color of her fair skin and light-color eyebrows that her hair color is natural.

"Are you ready?" I ask.

She reaches for her coffee cup off of the counter and says, "I am."

"Do you have your house keys?" I ask, looking at her other empty hand.

"No." She laughs. "You'd think this was a first for me, wouldn't you?" I watch as she walks back into her bedroom. I open the door leading to her store and wait for her to return. "Now I'm ready."

Looking around the small apartment, I ask, "Is this the only entrance to your apartment?"

She walks past me through the opened door. "No, there's a back entrance that leads to the alley. I suppose guests could use that door, but I just use this one to my store. I guess I haven't had enough company to use the other entrance yet."

As we walk through the shop, I notice that it's also decorated similar to her apartment. "Your shop's very quaint."

"Thank you. I'm pretty happy with the way it turned out."

We walk across the street and past the shops until we get to the sandy beaches. There's a slight chill in the air. Grace holds her coffee with both hands to warm them.

"I can see why Parker loves it here," I say, taking a sip of the hot java.

Her arm brushes against mine as we walk side by side.

"It's beautiful here, isn't it?"

"It is. I think it's odd that I've never been here before Parker moved here."

"I know, right? It's such a quaint place."

"I'm also surprised it's not swarmed with developers trying to buy up property to build condos."

"I'm sure one day it'll happen, but thankfully it hasn't happened yet."

We walk down by the water's edge while sipping the hot coffee. I spot a starfish near the shoreline. "Make a wish," I say to Grace.

"Why?"

"There's a starfish. It's supposed to be good luck to make a wish when you see one."

"Really? I never heard that."

"Make a wish before he leaves or I will," I tease, closing my eyes to make a wish. Since I've been on the island, I've been seeing signs that read, "Salty Kisses and Starfish Wishes." It must be true if it's in print.

"I need all the luck I can get."

I open my eyes and watch as she closes hers as if she's wishing upon a shooting star. I watch her closely as the waves overlap the shoreline. The moon is casting a soft glow on her face. She opens her eyes and smiles.

"What did you wish for?"

"If I tell you, then it won't come true," she teases.

There may be some truth to that if you're superstitious.

We walk a little further until we come to a bench near the fishing pier. I watch Grace as she sips her coffee. She's beautiful and I want to know more about her, but then I hear a woman scream. Her voice is frantic. I search the shoreline, but I don't see anyone or anything. It's just getting dark so it's a bit hard to see.

"Do you see anyone?" I ask, still searching the area.

Grace points to a couple who's near the street and away from the shoreline. "Over there," she says as she begins a fast walk in their direction. The man is lying down and the woman is kneeling beside him. They are an older couple, maybe in their seventies.

When I realize he may be unconscious, I increase my pace.

"What happened?"

"I think it's his heart," the elder woman cries.

"Does he have a history of heart problems?" I ask, kneeling on the other side of the man.

"He had a triple bypass two years ago."

I quickly assess him. "Grace, I need you to call 911 and tell them it's a possible heart attack and the victim is alive but unconscious. I then call Parker and tell him where we are and ask him to bring his medical bag."

"I didn't bring my phone," she says in a panic.

I hand her mine.

As I continue to assess the man, I say to the frail woman, "I'm a doctor and I think your husband is at risk of going into cardiac arrest." She places her trembling hands to her quivering lips. "Is he allergic to any medications?" She shakes her head as the tears stream down her pale face. "No. Nothing."

"When was his last attack?"

"Oh, dear," she stammers. "It was before his surgery, but I can't remember when. Three years ago."

I offer a small reassuring smile. I look up at Grace and she's still on the phone. "How old is your husband?"

"He's 72."

"I'm Dr. James Taylor. I run a family practice in Charlotte."

While I continue to assess the man, my plan is to keep the woman talking and her mind off of the situation with her loved one.

"I'm Clara."

I open each of the man's eyes to check his pupils for dilation.

"Are you visiting or do you live here?"

She stammers, "We're just here visiting."

"It's nice to meet you, Clara. Where are you visiting from?" I keep my fingers on the man's wrist so I can monitor his pulse rate. There isn't anything else I can do unless he goes into full cardiac arrest. Then he'll need C.P.R.

"We're from a town just on the outskirts of Charlotte. Walter and I came here to hunt for sea glass."

"Sea glass?" I ask. I've never heard of such a thing.

"It's just glass in the sea, but by the time it makes it to the seashore, the edges are smooth and it has a frosted appearance."

"I've never heard of it," I say honestly. "Do you and Walter have children?"

"Three."

Walter's pulse is getting weaker. "Do they live near you?" I hear heavy footsteps running down the sidewalk. I know without looking that it's Parker and probably Sarah, too.

"Sam does. Valerie and Victoria moved away right after college."

Clara stands and Parker kneels down across from me where Clara was kneeling and starts taking Walter's blood pressure. I tell him what I know while keeping my voice monotone. If I sound excited or anxious, it'll cause Clara to worry.

Parker looks at me with concern. My eyes travel to his blood pressure cuff and I see that Walter's blood pressure's dropping. The last thing I want to do in front of Clara is to perform C.P.R. on her husband. When C.P.R. is done correctly, ribs often break. I can hear the ambulance in the far distance. With luck it'll arrive before Walter goes into full cardiac arrest.

No such luck. It looks like Walter's going into full cardiac arrest.

Since Walter's an older man, I ask his wife, "Does your husband have a D.N.R.?"

"What's that?"

"Do not resuscitate. If he needs C.P.R., is it okay to perform it?"

"No, he doesn't have a living will with a D.N.R. We never got around to doing it. Please save him," she pleads.

Parker and I perform two-person C.P.R. on the elderly gentleman. Just before the ambulance arrives, Walter is breathing and has a faint pulse.

I'm relieved that the ambulance arrives quickly. Although Charlotte is the closest large city to the island, several small towns are between here and there. The ambulance came from one of those towns. Parker and I stay with Clara as she relays the information needed for them to treat Walter. "Do you want me to call your son and have him meet you at the hospital?"

"Oh, thank you, doctor. That would be wonderful since I don't have any way of contacting him."

I get Sam's phone number from Clara and then help her into the front of the ambulance. Normally patients ride in the back with their loved ones but because of her age, she'll be more comfortable in the front seat with the driver.

It takes the E.M.S. workers a few minutes to pull off as they're probably inserting an IV line for medications and fluids into Walter's arm. Hopefully, he won't need more C.P.R.

I call Clara and Walter's son, Sam, and then Sarah, Parker, Grace, and I return to Grace's house for a nightcap. In the medical field, at the end of your shift you always have a pass down or sometimes it's called a give report. It's where you pass down information that's happened on your shift to the oncoming shift. Law enforcement does the same thing.

They call it debriefing. It helps the oncoming shift get an idea of what's going on, but it also serves as an outlet for the off-going shift. It's a chance to unwind and it gives you a release from a strenuous shift.

Not that this was bad for Parker and me, but it was traumatic for Clara and maybe even for Grace and Sarah.

Grace opens a bottle of red wine and pours four glasses. "I can't believe how calm you were doing all that," she says, handing me a glass. "I was freaking out when 911 asked me questions I didn't have the answers to."

"Nothing good comes from a hysterical doctor." I reach for another glass of wine and follow her into the other room where Parker and Sarah are waiting.

"I suppose you're right," she says with a smile.

When the wine's gone I leave with Sarah and Parker, but I let them get halfway down the stairs before saying my goodbyes to Grace. I wanted to get to know her on a personal level and perhaps ask her out, but the timing isn't right to do that now.

"Thank you for a memorable evening," she teases with a smile.

"I'm sorry about that. I didn't have anything planned for this evening, but I wasn't expecting that to happen."

"I still had a good time." *She did?* "Except for the emergency," she says.

"James, are you coming?" Sarah asks from the bottom of the stairs.

"I'm on my way." I turn my attention back to Grace. "I need to get going."

"Have a good night, James."

"You, too, Grace."

***

The next morning, Parker asks, "Dad, what were you doing with Grace last night?"

"What do you mean?" I reach for the pot of coffee to refill my cup.

"You're not seeing her, are you?"

I sit at the table across from him and he looks serious. I'm a grown man and this comes as a surprise to me.

"Would that bother you if I were?"

Parker holds his coffee mug close to his lips. "I take it you're considering asking her out."

I say honestly, "We were just having coffee. It wasn't a big deal."

"You were walking on the beach together. And you still haven't answered my question."

"No, Parker. I'm not considering asking her out, but why would that bother you?" It's a lie, but I can see concern in my son's eyes.

He pauses to take a breath. "Maybe because Sarah and I will be married and Grace will be my mother-in-law, you'll be Sarah's father-in-law, and that'll make us all family… sort of."

I laugh. I will be Sarah's father-in-law, but Grace and I won't be related in any way. However, I understand his concern and if he'll feel awkward, then I'll need to maintain a friendly relationship with her.

"You have nothing to worry about, Parker."

"I hope not."

He doesn't. This isn't Iceland. It has a small population, so the country maintains a genealogical database that people can check to make sure they aren't dating someone too closely related to them. No one wants a *Game of Thrones* situation where someone unknowingly dates their aunt. If people from Iceland aren't careful, someone could end up being his own grandpa. I'm sure I can be Sarah's father-in-law and her stepfather, if things should work out that way.

Parker looks over at me and asks, "So whatever happened with that problem you had at work with Anna and Matt?"

"Anna filed a sexual harassment complaint against Matt."

"I hate to hear that."

"Me, too."

"Do you think it's true?"

"Who knows? Unless there's a witness, it's a 'he said, she said' situation. I like him and I find it hard to believe he could be guilty of anything like this." I exhale loudly. "Hell, I like her, too, and I can't imagine that she would make something like this up."

"What does she have to gain from this?"

"I don't know. Nothing."

Parker sighs. "Sexual harassment can be anything from inappropriate words to inappropriate touching. What did Matt say about this?"

"When I called him into the office to talk to him about it, he put in his resignation effective immediately."

"What?"

I run my hands through my hair and look out the opened window. "It's true. He said he was innocent and she was manipulative." I look back at Parker. "Before I could ask him anything else, he stood up and left."

"What did he mean by she's manipulative?"

"I wish I knew."

"If you were innocent, wouldn't you stay and fight?"

"I can't answer that. It would be hard to prove either way. Maybe he didn't want the hassle of it all."

"I didn't know either of them very well, but what I did know about him I really liked."

"He was a hell of a worker and he'll be hard to replace."

Parker says, standing to rinse out his coffee cup, "This story makes me grateful that I have all women working for me."

CHAPTER 2

JAMES

When Parker and Sarah leave for work, I shower and head out to explore the quaint island. I remember what Clara said about sea glass, so I decide to try to find some after breakfast. Later in the day, I'll also call the hospital to check on Walter.

I decide to have a breakfast sandwich and coffee at the only market on the island. The island is owned by a widower named Tony. His son is the island's preacher who also happens to be married to Grace's other daughter, Carly.

"Hello, doctor. It's good seeing you this fine morning," Tony says, using his strong Italian voice.

"Good morning, Tony. You can call me James."

"Oh, yes. I must remember that. What can I get for you this morning?"

"Sarah said that you make breakfast sandwiches," I say, walking closer to the deli counter where he's standing.

"Best on the island." He laughs.

I wonder if he's laughing because they're the only breakfast sandwiches on the island or if they're really that good. "I'll take one with egg and sausage and a black coffee, please."

"Coming right up."

"Take your time, I'm in no hurry."

I notice that Tony uses Jimmy Dean sausage, which is good sausage. Jimmy Dean won a Grammy for "Big Bad John," and when he was young, he made sausage with his grandfather. He once said, "I used to help my granddaddy make sausage. He would mix it up in a cleaned-out washtub with his hands, no gloves. Man, if we did anything like that today, they would jack the jail up and throw us under it." I love Jimmy Dean sausage, and I bet I would love his grandfather's sausage.

I browse the market while Tony prepares the sandwich. Carly and Beau walk into the market. Tony gets excited when he sees his son and daughter-in-law. Then he stands on his tiptoes so he can look beyond the counter.

"What? No grandbabies?" Tony asks. Beau and Carly have two daughters, Myra and Maria.

"Gram and Pap are watching them today."

"That's nice," Tony says as he cuts my sandwich in half and wraps it up.

I walk up to the counter to pay for my purchase. Carly looks at me with a smile. "Hi, I didn't see you here."

"How are you this morning?" I ask, looking at Beau and then at his wife.

"Fine. I'm heading to the bookstore and Beau's heading to the church. Thought we'd stop in for some breakfast since the girls are with their great-grandparents."

I nod as I pay for my purchase. "You can join me if you'd like."

She looks back at Beau. Not for his permission but to see if he has other plans. "Okay, we'd like that."

During breakfast, I ask them about sea glass.

"Beau has the perfect place to search for sea glass. He has several storage containers full of it in our home."

I look from Carly to Beau.

"It's true. I've been collecting it most of my life."

"And yet I find it strange I'm just now learning about it and I'm what… fifty…ish."

Carly and Beau laugh. "Unless you live near the water or visit it frequently, you probably wouldn't know about sea glass."

"I suppose not."

"But if you go down Shell Lane towards our house, you're bound to find what you're looking for there. You can park at our house and walk down the shoreline. You'll know the spot when you see it."

Carly adds, "It's where the waves pick up. It's at the very tip of the island."

"Thank you. I'll head down that way later."

"What else do you have planned for today?" Carly looks at me with her big brown eyes. She doesn't have the blond hair that her sister and mother have. I'm assuming she must look like her father. She and Beau make an attractive couple; both have dark hair and features.

Should I tell her I plan on visiting her mother's candle shop today? "I was actually planning on visiting some of the shops on Shell Lane today. See if I can find any unique gifts to take back home with me."

"Well, if you need help shopping you can always stop by the bookstore. Carly will be able to guide you in the right direction." Beau gives Carly a teasing smile.

"That's true, I will," she says. "And if I'm not busy, I may even take you there myself."

Finishing off my coffee, I say, "I'll keep that in mind. If you'll excuse me, I need to get going and beat the crowds. I hear the beaches can get pretty busy by noon." I stand and thank Tony before heading out.

On my way to the beach, I call Clara and Walter's son, Sam, to check on Walter's condition.

"Sam here," he answers.

"Sam, it's Doctor Taylor. I called you last night about your father. I'm just calling to see how he's doing this morning."

"My father passed away on the way to the hospital. They tried to revive him, but they said there was nothing they could do for him."

A lump immediately forms in my throat. This isn't what I expected to hear, but of course he was old. "I'm sorry. How's your mother and sisters?"

"As well as they can be. My sisters are both traveling home, and Mom and I are heading out now to make his funeral arrangements."

"Okay. I won't keep you. I'm sorry the outcome wasn't better."

"Thank you, Doctor Taylor. Can I get your address please? Mom wants to send you a thank you note for everything you did for Dad and her last night."

"That's not necessary."

"Please, she wants to do this."

"Okay." I rattle off my address before hanging up.

I wish I could have done more. I think back to make sure I did everything I could for him.

GRACE

I couldn't sleep last night from thinking about that poor man and woman, Clara and Walter. That poor sweet woman and the worried and frightened look on her face as her husband lay helpless on the sidewalk. I was scared and was praying he would be all right. It definitely helped me when Parker and Sarah showed up. Although Parker was busy helping his father, Sarah was my support as we held hands with Clara and watched helplessly.

In the morning as I open the doors to the shop, I see James standing across the street holding his phone up to his ear. I smile and wave, but it looks like he's in deep conversation although he offers a slight wave. I find it surprising how much I've thought about him since Christmas. He's the first man since my husband that I've ever looked at a second time, much less thought about.

Parker's pretty amazing, so I should have known his father would be also. Sarah told me this morning about the story of how Parker's mother got pregnant with him while they were both in college and she left without ever telling him she was pregnant with his child. From what Sarah said, she didn't do it because she was being hateful, she did it out of love. She didn't want him to drop out of college because of an unexpected pregnancy. Then she died when Parker was in his teens and he was then sent to a children's home to live until they were able to locate his missing father. Sarah said James never committed to a serious relationship after Parker's mother left him. He was heartbroken and never really got over her. A bit like me, I suppose. I never dated after Michael's death. Maybe people have only one true love in their lifetime. One soulmate. With all of the billions of people in the world, I find this hard to believe. Yet here are two people, both in their fifties, who have loved only once. It's sad, isn't it?

I light a few candles in the store, play some bohemian music, and wait for my first customer. It's still early so I don't expect a crowd until later. Some people on vacation like to sleep in and relax while others are up early and want to see as much of the island as they can during their time here. I'm surprised and excited to see my first customer is James.

He peeks his head in and looks around. "Did I beat the rush?" He smiles a devilishly handsome grin.

"You did. Please, come in," I say, waving him inside the already opened door.

He walks in and looks around. "Does it always smell this good in here?" he asks, inhaling deeply.

"I hope so, especially since my business is selling scented candles." Walking towards him, I smile. "What brings you in here this time of morning?" I can't smell the candles as much as I can smell his cologne. He smells of spice, sandalwood, and musk.

"I had breakfast with your daughter and thought I would search for this sea glass everyone is talking about."

"How is Sarah?" I ask, straightening the stack of books written by Carly. I know Sarah's well since I just saw her this morning.

"She's good, but I was talking about Carly."

"Ah. You must have had breakfast at the market."

"I did. It was quite delicious by the way. Anyway, she and Beau came in and joined me." We both look out the window and watch as Beau and Carly walk toward the bookstore. He holds her hand as they walk across the tree-lined street. "I must tell you that both of your daughters are quite charming."

"Thank you. I think so, too."

"I didn't know their father, but I can see a lot of their mother in the way they look and act."

I blush at the compliment. I don't know if he meant for it to be a compliment, but that's how I took it. "Thank you, that's very sweet of you to say. Carly looks and acts a lot like her father."

"I'm only speaking the truth." He's pauses as if he's in deep thought or maybe he thinks I'm an idiot for blushing like a young schoolgirl over nothing. I turn my back to him so he can't see the rose color in my cheeks. "You know, I'm here for only a few more days. I was wondering if you'd like to go out with me on Friday. Maybe we can go to Charlotte for dinner. I can show you around. You can see my home and my office, and I can show you some of the landmarks that make Charlotte such a great area."

It takes me only a second to reply. I turn around to face him, rosy-colored cheeks and all, and say, "I'd love to."

JAMES

I know Parker asked me not to get too close to Sarah's mom, but he obviously has no idea how hard this is. I didn't mean to lie to him and maybe, hopefully, he'll forgive me quickly. Grace is kind, beautiful, charming, and all those other things a man looks for in a woman. Plus, she naturally smells of vanilla and cinnamon. Well, maybe it's not natural but she always smells of the same delectable scent. It's not like I asked for her hand in marriage. It's just a date, for God's sake. Surely, he can't be too upset over that, can he?

"Good. What time should I pick you up?"

"I don't close the shop until 5 o'clock. It may be too late by then."

"I guess it depends on what time you want to get back. The city of Charlotte is breathtaking after dark. Or we can go make a full day of it on Saturday. It's up to you."

She bites the inside of her cheek as if in deep thought. Maybe she doesn't want to be with me late at night on a Friday. Friday is definitely a date night for couples. Married or single. If she chooses Saturday, that would guarantee an entire day with her, which means more time I get to spend with her. If Parker is too upset that I asked Grace out, then this could be our one and only time together. I won't hurt my son. Not if he's adamant about me not spending time with his future mother-in-law. No matter how ridiculous his reasoning is.

"I usually keep late night hours so Friday will be good for me. That is, if it's good for you?"

She chose the date night. "Perfect. I'll pick you up at seven o'clock then?"

"I'll be ready."

"Good. I'm looking forward to it."

"Me, too."

I purchase a few candles although Grace tries to just give them to me before leaving. I do some window-shopping before heading back to Parker's house to drop off the candles before heading down to the beach to search for sea glass. My mind drifts off to my phone call with Sam earlier. I hate hearing that Walter didn't make it. As doctors and medical professionals, we do our best but sometimes it's not in God's plan. I hope that his wife, Clara, can manage without him.

***

I'm pleasantly surprised at the sea glass I found just down from Beau and Carly's house. I can't say it's something I'd like to do on a regular basis, but being in the sunshine and in the water was very therapeutic for my soul.

I wash the salt water off of the smooth, frosty-colored glass and shower before Parker and Sarah get home from work. I need to decide how I'm going to tell him about my plans with Grace this weekend. Maybe I should tell him with Sarah there. No. Wait. What if she isn't thrilled with the idea either? But Sarah's mother has been alone for a long time, so certainly Sarah will be happy to see her mother gradually claim the life she's missed since her husband's death. Parker would be happy for me as long as it wasn't with his future mother-in-law.

I decide to go for a walk while I wait. When I see Carly in the bookstore alone, I decide to go in there. With her back to me, she says, "We're closing in fifteen minutes."

I stop while holding the door open. "I can come back tomorrow."

She turns around and looks at me while offering me a kind smile. "Don't be silly. Come on in."

Still standing at the door, I say, "I don't want to hold you up."

"Please. Come in. We're nearly family." *We're nearly family?* Those words stop me. Maybe asking Grace out *was* a bad idea. She walks over to me and tugs my arm until I walk inside. "I didn't want someone coming in thinking they had hours to browse." While closing the door behind me, she adds, "Although if I didn't have a family to get home to, I would probably let them shop until they were done."

"I saw that you were still opened and thought I'd come in."

"I'm glad you did." She walks back behind the counter. "Did you find any sea treasures today?"

"Sea treasures?"

"You know, things from the sea. Shells, starfish, driftwood, sand dollars, sea glass. Things like that?"

"I did. You were right in guiding me to that location."

"So you found some sea glass?"

"I found several pieces actually."

"We used to search for that a lot when Sarah and I were little. Mom, Gram, and Pap would pack a huge picnic lunch and we'd go out for the entire day searching for sea treasures."

"It sounds like a great childhood you and your sister had."

"It was. After our father died, Gram and Pap stepped up and helped Mom a lot."

"I'm sorry that you lost your father," I say honestly.

"Thank you," she says sadly. "I feel sorrier for Mom. I don't remember much about him. But Mom lost her husband, friend, and the father of her children, leaving her broken and alone to raise two young daughters." She wipes away a tear. "Why am I even telling you this? I'm sorry. Sometimes I just ramble on for no known reason."

I decide I should ask her for advice about taking her mother out. Or maybe I should ask Sarah? No, that would be too weird or maybe I'm fearful she'll share the same views as my son. "Can I ask you something?"

She looks up from opening the register to count the money. "Sure," she says, a little surprised. "You can ask me anything."

"When I came in, you mentioned I was welcome near closing time because we're nearly family."

"I did. Did that make you feel weird?"

"No, but what did you mean by that?"

"Just that Sarah's marrying Parker and you're Parker's dad. You'll be related to my sister, so I just assumed we'd all be related in a round-about way."

"I see." I rub my hand over my scruffy beard. "I have another question."

"Okay," she says, closing the register drawer.

"If I were to take your mother out, would that be strange for you?"

Carly smiles. "You asked my mom out?"

"I may have. Would that bother you if I had?"

Carly steps away from the register and walks closer to me. "No, not at all. I'd be thrilled."

That's good to know. Relieved, I ask, "What do you think your sister would think?"

"I can't answer for my sister, but I know that Mom's been alone for a long time. I can't imagine Sarah would mind."

"Even with her marrying my son? Like you said, we'll be family."

"Yeah, but it's just a date. You didn't ask our mom to marry you, did you?" She doesn't let me answer. "And anyways, you'll be an in-law to Sarah. No blood between either of you. Huge difference. But you're a doctor, you don't need me telling you this." Before I can say anything, she says, "Oh, I get it. Parker's bothered by this?"

"He doesn't know."

"But he warned you about asking her out, didn't he?"

I raise a brow. "How could you know this?"

"You and Mom exchanged a look, or several looks, or maybe it was your body language at the Christmas Eve party. I'm not sure but whoever witnessed it, we all must have thought the same thing."

"And what was that?"

"That you both were attracted to each other."

GRACE

I feel like a schoolgirl on her first date. I had Sarah and Carly come over to help me choose the right outfit for tomorrow. I've been married for God's sake so why am I so nervous about a date? Because I haven't been out with someone in… well, let's just say a very long time.

I soon realize maybe Mom would have been a better choice to help me. Carly wants me to dress like a nun or perhaps a schoolteacher and Sarah wants me to dress like a lady of the night. I'm no prude, but even I know when too much is too much. But I do have to admit they have excellent taste in shoes, handbags, and jewelry. I decide to keep my date attire to myself. Neither one would approve, but I now know my outfit of choice is the right one. I can change my mind, of course.

"Are you girls sure you're okay with James and me going out?"

Sarah and Carly look at each other and laugh.

"Yeah, Mom. This is way overdue. I was beginning to think you would never date. Who knew it'd be with Parker's dad?" Carly says, laughing.

I turn serious. This was a fear of mine, although I never discussed it with anyone. "Does that bother either of you?" I sit on the bed where the shoes, purses, and jewelry are strung about. Carly's at the foot of the bed while Sarah's sitting on the chair at the vanity.

"We already told you your dating is long past due."

"No, not that." I look at Sarah. "Does my dating James bother you or Parker?"

"Doesn't bother me. I like James and he's a great guy."

"But it bothers Parker?"

Carly and I both turn our attention to Sarah.

"This is the thing about Parker." She tightens her ponytail and faces the both of us. "He's afraid if this doesn't work out there will be an awkwardness between the families and he doesn't want that."

"I can understand that," I admit

"And —" she begins.

"What? There's more?" Now this concerns me. Parker must really be bothered by this.

"He says if this does work out and y'all have kids, it'll be all sorts of jacked up." Carly starts laughing and Sarah laughs with her. "Our kids and your and James' kids will be brother and sisters."

Now I laugh. "They will not and you will *never* have to worry about that."

"No, Sarah," Carly says still laughing. "Their kids will be your kids' aunts and uncles like Beau and I would be."

"So, if they have kids later than us…" Sarah tries to say still laughing before I interrupt.

"Okay. I'm not having any more children. Ever. And I doubt James wants more children at his age. This conversation is moot. But please tell me Parker isn't really concerned about this, is he?"

Sarah sits up and her smile fades. "He just doesn't want any ill feelings or awkwardness if this doesn't work."

My children and their happiness come first. "Maybe I should call James and tell him I'm having second thoughts."

Sarah says, "That won't do any good."

"Why won't it?"

"Parker told his dad not to ask you out, but he did anyway. I guess you're just too irresistible."

I'm not sure why I get some pleasure from hearing this, but I do.

We clean up and lay the shoes, purse, and jewelry I decided to wear off to the side. I'd like to talk to Parker before my date tomorrow. If this isn't okay with him, then I'll tell James this is a bad idea. Surely, he'll understand. When Carly and Sarah leave, I have a glass of red wine before going to bed.

I wake up the next morning in a great mood. After Michael's death I finally feel like I'm living again. The date with James tonight has nothing to do with it. This feeling is all thanks to my parents that I have my own home, a respectable and enjoyable job, and a life. I have a life. I didn't know how much I missed it until recently.

Today, I shower first and then have my coffee on the balcony. It's the dawn of a new day and I'm so grateful to be here to enjoy it. I'm not the only one. The joggers and the early-morning walkers are also taking advantage of the day that was given to them. I see Tony across the street and give him a friendly wave and a smile. My heart hurts for his loss of his dear wife, Maria. Although her passing was a few years ago, I know the feelings are still raw inside him. It took me decades to move on with my life. Will Tony get a second chance at love? Is there time for him? I hope so. We're nearly the same age, he has lots of time to find love.

Mom and Dad come into the shop today just like they do every day. Mom stays and helps me out while Dad goes over to the market to have lunch and to visit with Tony.

"Are you nervous about your date tonight?"

Mom always was one to say exactly what she was thinking.

"Nervous, excited, nervous, scared, nervous," I say with a laugh, repeating the word "nervous."

"You have nothing to be nervous about."

"It's been a long time since I've been out with anyone."

"It's just dinner with a friend," she says, straightening up some candles in the corner cupboard.

"Is that what it'll be like? My nervous stomach says otherwise."

"Probably not." She giggles. "But you'll be fine. Have you decided what to wear yet?"

"I have. Carly and Sarah came over last night and helped me."

"Oh, Lord. I can only imagine what they chose for you."

"They were actually a big help. I decided to not wear anything they suggested."

"You know," she says, turning around to straighten another section of the store. "Vintage dresses never go out of style. Lucille Ball and Audrey Hepburn are class acts. People forget this, but Lucy was a glamour model before she became a comic actress."

I recall searching online for dresses and Mom's right. There was a lot of new apparel made to look vintage from that time era. There was never a scandal or talk about those women dressing sleazy or sleeping their way to the top. Audrey, however, once posed for an ad early in her career in which she wore a padded bra. She signed a copy of the photo used in the ad "Audrey — and friends." Two class acts: I mean Lucy and Audrey, of course. That's the look I'm going for: classy.

"I know whatever you decide, you'll be stunning in it."

"Thank you, Mom."

"I'm so happy for you. I almost want your dad to bring me over here before your date tonight so I can take pictures of the two love birds."

A memory flashes before me of my and Michael's junior and senior prom. I can't tell you how much film they used taking pictures of us, of me alone, and of Michael by himself. Michael never minded being in front of the camera. He also enjoyed spending hours upon hours looking through photo albums. Now that he's gone, I'm thankful for the abundance of photos I have of him and us.

"Oh, God. Please don't."

Mom laughs. "I wouldn't do that."

"And we're not love birds. It's just two friends having dinner. Remember?"

"Whatever it is I just want you to have a great time."

I close the shop earlier than usual so I have enough time to get ready. I still haven't talked to Parker, but I'll make sure to mention this to James sometime this evening.

I take a bubble bath and listen to soothing music to help relax me. While I dress, I decide some red wine might help calm my nerves. I shouldn't be this nervous. It's just dinner with a man I know. That's all.

After talking with Mom, I decide on a vintage style black dress with black heels and a black clutch. I also decide to pair it with a single strand of pearls and pearl earrings. These are some of the accessories my daughters helped me pick out. With nervous hands I try to clasp the necklace without success. Taking some deep breaths, I try it again. No luck.

James arrives just a few minutes earlier than I expected. With the pearl necklace dangling in my hand, I answer the door. He's standing there in a black suit, crisp white shirt with cuff links, and a black tie with a tie clip. He looks like he could be going to a black-tie event. He offers a smile, and I admit to myself that he's extremely handsome.

"You look beautiful." He looks at me with appreciation.

"Thank you. You do, too."

"These are for you." I smile when I notice the large bouquet of red roses with baby breaths he's holding out in front of him.

"Thank you and please, come in," I say, opening the door wider for him to step through.

"I stopped and got the flowers and yet I'm still early."

"You're just on time," I say, closing the door behind me. "Let me get these in water before we leave."

I walk into the kitchen in search of a vase while he stands at the bar watching me. I set the pearls down while I fill the vase with water and put the roses in the vase. Once the flowers are neatly arranged, I set them in the middle of the table. "Beautiful," I say while looking at the stunning floral arrangement.

"Yes, you are," he says barely above a whisper.

Since I'm not sure he intended me to hear him, I decide to ignore his comment. I walk back over to him and pick up the single strand of pearls. "I was going to wear these, but I can't get the clasp to cooperate."

"May I?" he asks, reaching for the strand of pearls from my hands.

My heart picks up its pace. Without saying a word, I lift my shoulder-length hair and turn around. Goosebumps creep up my body at the closeness we share. I inhale his cologne and close my eyes. God, he smells heavenly. When the necklace is clasped, he lightly touches my neck where the necklace rests before trailing his fingers ever so lightly down my shoulder. I take a step forward and try desperately to get my breathing under control. It's been a long time since someone's touched me like that. It's also been a long time since someone's looked at me like that. Is it wrong to say that I've missed it?

"Thank you." I turn around, offering him my best smile.

"Are you ready?"

"I am."

As we walk down the steps to his car, I almost expect to see Carly and Sarah, or Mom and Dad walking down the street. I'm relieved when I don't see anyone. James opens the door for me and it allows me a few seconds to calm my nerves before he gets into the driver's seat. What will we talk about? Is he as nervous as I am? He appears to be cool and calm. Maybe I'm not ready for this.

As we pull out of the driveway, he says, "I wasn't sure what kind of food you liked so I made dinner reservations at two places."

"That was thoughtful."

He looks over and smiles. "I wanted to give you the options of the best seafood or the best steak that Charlotte has to offer."

"That's a tough choice."

"That's why *you're* making the decision."

I laugh. "Oh, the pressure of a first date." As I ponder this, I ask, "I'm assuming you like both of the choices you're offering."

"I do. You can't go wrong with either food choice or either restaurant for that matter."

"To be honest, there's a plethora of seafood on the island and it's been a while since I had a good steak."

People can definitely get tired of seafood. In his vaudeville days, Groucho Marx once performed for a while at a theater whose manager provided room and board. The manager was thrifty and kept a net in the ocean near the theater. Groucho's breakfast, lunch, and dinner swam into that net. After the engagement at the theater was over, Groucho ate nothing but beef for a week.

"Steak sounds good to me. Would you mind calling the seafood restaurant and cancelling the reservations?"

"No, of course not."

"My phone's in the console." He tells me the name of the reservation and reminds me again that his last name's Taylor, not Blake, like his son's. Once I cancel the reservation, he says, "I have to tell you, I'm a bit nervous about this evening." I appreciate his honesty. "It's been awhile since I've dated. So, if I do or say something stupid, I'll be blaming it on that."

"I'm so nervous, I probably won't even notice."

He glances at me quickly. "We're a pair, aren't we?"

"I guess we are."

The drive to the restaurant is nearly an hour. I guess we could use this time to get to know each other. How much of my non-existent life do I want to share with him? In the last twenty-something years of my life I wasn't even living. I was going through the motions — and not feeling emotions — and that was it. For the past twenty-something years of my life, I have been guilty of self-imposed loneliness.

When I remain silent, he says, "From the few moments I've been in your shop, is it safe to say that you like calypso music?"

"I mostly play it for the patrons. Most are on vacation and the music has a tropical feel. Relaxing and happy. Who doesn't like that? But my personal choice would be country."

He asks with a smile, "Josh Turner? Garth Brooks? Tim McGraw? Faith Hill? Conway Twitty?"

"You're a fan, too, I see."

"All my life."

I watch as he turns on the radio to a country music station. "Do you sing, too?" I ask.

"I line dance, but I'm really not much of a singer. But that's never stopped me from singing karaoke from time to time."

"You line dance and sing karaoke?"

He looks at me in amazement. "You don't?"

"No. I never have." Michael and I used to do a lot of things but since his death, I focused on getting out of bed and caring for my girls. I've missed out on so much.

"There's a country bar I frequent on occasion. We can go there next weekend. I think you'll like it. It's a great way to unwind and just have a good time with good people."

He's already planning a next date. How do I feel about that? Those good bumps — I mean goosebumps — creep up my spine again. I think I like the thought of seeing him again. "It sounds like fun."

It's been a long time since I dated and since I've been intimate with anyone. How will this work? I mean, I used to not have to worry about safe sex. It was just another advantage to having a life-long partner.

If and when I do decide to make love to a man, will he spend the night? Will we make love and then he leaves to return home? Will I be the one returning home? Will I be a one-night stand? What if he wants to be intimate and I don't? What if I forgot how? STOP IT, GRACE! You're being foolish. If and when it happens I know it'll be perfect. I hope it'll be perfect. Why am I having these thoughts? Making love to James has never crossed my mind. Until now. How soon is too soon to make love to someone? I guess that depends on who you ask. I have no doubt that Carly and Sarah will have very different answers. Michael and I waited a long time, but that was because we were both virgins and afraid. Well, I was afraid; he was anxious to see if it was as great as he'd heard about. And James? When was his last time? A year ago? A month ago? A week ago? I hope not. What about safe sex? Will I need to have a supply of condoms in my nightstand drawer? Do I offer them like mints? Do I put them in a pretty glass bowl and say, "Here, choose a color, a texture, and a size." I laugh to myself. I am way over thinking this. I need another glass of wine, or maybe that's my problem. Maybe I had one glass too many. Or maybe my problem is that all of my orgasms for the past twenty-two years have been self-caused.

CHAPTER 3

JAMES

I made plans for next week without even asking her first. I should have at least asked her out before planning on going to a karaoke place with her. I'm such an idiot. I was waiting for her to say something other than what she said. Like, "Whoa, buddy. You're moving kind of fast, don't ya think?" Or "You're moving like you're in the Indianapolis 500 when you're really in a school zone." Or "You're pretty sure of yourself. What makes you think I'd go out with you again?" Or "Arrogant much? Can we see how this date goes first?" I never expected "It sounds like fun." I like the idea of knowing we have another date secured. I can already tell one date with her won't be enough. I also like the fact that she's so laid back and we seem to have some things in common.

I decide now might be a good time to change the subject before she changes her mind. She also doesn't seem to want to talk much about herself, I need to find something that she likes to talk about. Maybe then she'll want to open up about other parts of her life. "Can I ask what got you into the candle business? I know how you acquired the shop, but how did you get into making candles and the other craft items?"

I can see her visibly relax.

"After I got married money was tight. I love candles so I experimented and taught myself how to make my own. Word spread quickly in our small town in Virginia and I started turning a small profit selling candles and some craft items to neighbors and friends. Then when Michael and I had the girls, I opened a small business."

"But eventually you closed it."

"I did. After Michael's death and I wasn't able to keep it up."

"I'm sorry to hear that."

"Thank you. I got depressed and moved in with my parents. They insisted so they could help me look out for the girls while keeping a close eye on me as well. I guess they saw the extent of my depression before I did."

"And you've lived with them ever since?" I hope I don't sound like I'm judging her.

"For the next twenty-two years. I didn't need to work; my husband left us well off. It's probably a good thing as I was too depressed to function on some days."

"Sadly, I can relate to a degree."

"You can?"

"Not about everything you've been through. But Parker's mom was also killed, I think I already told you that."

"You've mentioned it before."

"But did you know that she got pregnant with Parker while we were in college?"

"I vaguely remember something about this." Sarah told me but I don't mention that.

"I was in med school. We were planning on marrying, but when she learned about the pregnancy, she left. I had no idea where she was and I also didn't learn about Parker until well after his birth."

"That explains the different last names."

I glance over and there's a sadness in her eyes. "He has his mother's last name. He was a teenager before I learned that I even had a child."

"How did he find you?"

"He didn't. After her death, there weren't any known living family members, so Parker was sent to a children's home to live. He was an adolescent and would probably never be adopted." I get choked up at the thought of my son being there. "Bea, the woman who runs the home, found me."

"I'm sorry. I had no idea."

"Thank you. I'm sorry, too, but it's in the past."

"Is this the same home that Parker and Sarah visit every Tuesday?"

"It is. They are both a blessing to the children."

"You also donate your time there."

"I do. They did a lot for my son in my absence." I focus my attention on my driving because I don't want to show her the pain on my own face at the memory. "But I guess my point is that I can relate to your loss. Not that Parker's mom, Kara, and I were married, but I never moved on without her. I've dated here and there, but I never found anyone as special as she was." I pull up to the valet at the restaurant and I'm glad to get away from such a deep conversation. I look over at her and I swear her eyes are glistening with unshed tears. I offer her my best smile. "Stay in the car and I'll get your door for you."

I offer Grace my hand and she takes it. We're immediately led to our table. The thing I've learned in my life is to not be a hurry. I try hard to enjoy the experiences along the way. Those include meals, travel, and leisure.

I've been here enough times that I don't need to read over the menu to know what's on it or to know what I want. I'm a creature of habit. I like what I like. I do admire the view as I watch Grace peruse the menu. As she scans it, she looks over the menu at me watching her before browsing it again. About the third time, I smile. She folds up the leather menu before she sets it on the white linen tablecloth.

"What are you doing?" she asks with a smile.

"Admiring the view."

She looks around the room. "It is beautiful here."

"That's not the view I'm talking about."

She blushes. "You're embarrassing me."

"You're beautiful."

"You're embarrassing me."

I watch as she fidgets with the white linen napkin on her lap. "I'm sorry. I'll try to not mention your beauty any more this evening."

She lets out a small laugh. "You already know what you want?" I raise a brow at her question. There's something about double-meaning questions, when asked by a beautiful woman, that makes the conversation interesting. "To eat," she adds with a laugh.

"I've been here before. I already know the menu."

The server comes and takes our drink order. While Grace orders wine, I chose water as my beverage of choice. "You're not drinking?"

"Only because I'm driving. I'll have a night cap later when we return on the island."

She picks up her water glass. "I will, too, then. I'd hate to see you drink alone." I watch in amusement as she takes a sip of her cold water.

"You're still nervous?"

She sets the glass down and readjusts her linen napkin and says, "I'm so nervous. I know it's absurd. I feel like a schoolgirl on her first date. Ever. In her whole entire life." I get the picture. She lays the napkin on her lap again while smiling a nervous smile.

"I think it's cute," I admit. I think she's cute and so is everything about her.

Before she can say anything, the server brings Grace her wine. "Are you ready to order?"

I look at Grace and she tells me to order first. I have a shrimp cocktail for starters, a salad with balsamic vinaigrette, a petit filet cooked medium, and a side order of fresh green beans.

Grace tells the server, "I'll have the same."

Although it's a great choice, I want to make sure this is what she wants. "They have other salad dressings if you'd like to try one of their house brands. Or a different side dish, perhaps."

She looks at the server and then to me. "I'm fine."

The server leaves and I haven't forgotten about her being nervous. I wonder if this is why she ordered exactly what I did. Or maybe she likes everything that I ordered. "If there's something on your dinner plate you don't like, we can always send it back and get you something else."

"No. It sounds perfect. It was like you were ordering for me."

"Good. I've never had a bad meal here or bad service."

"That's my kind of restaurant." She clears her throat. "About what we were talking about in the car. I'm really sorry about Parker and the loss of his mother."

"Thank you." I release a long breath. "I'm thankful that it all worked out. His mother's loss is still tragic, but it brought Parker and me together and that's what's important. He's incredible and I can't imagine my life without him." I'm still very much angry with her for keeping my son away from me.

"He is amazing and I'm excited that Sarah found him."

"I feel the same way. She's just what Parker needed."

"Speaking of Parker and Sarah." She takes a sip of her wine. And by her tone, I now wish I had an alcoholic beverage in front in me. "Did Parker voice any concerns about this… about us going out?"

Either she already knows the answer or Sarah has a problem with us dating, and I know for a fact that Sarah's fine with this. I recall the last conversation I had with Parker and he has voiced his concerns more than once. He warned me not to get too close to her.

"He may have mentioned that this might be weird for him."

"And yet you asked me out anyway?"

"You obviously have no idea how hard you are to resist," I say honestly. I see a blush on her cheeks. "I tried to stay away but then I realized Parker's concerns are ridiculous." I decide to continue before she agrees with him. "We're not biological family. Even after Parker and Sarah marry, you and I are still not biological family."

"Was that his only concern?"

"Yes. He's never mentioned anything else bothering him. I thought that was enough."

"He's never mentioned anything about us having children to you?"

I nearly choke. "Kids? Me? Us? At my age?" I laugh. "No. I can honestly say this isn't a concern and if it is, he never led me to believe it was. And trust me when I say that Parker would tell me. He rarely holds his feelings back and when I say rarely, I mean never." I look at her and she is now laughing. "Did Sarah say something?"

"My Sarah has quite an imagination."

"What did she say?"

"Nothing worth repeating."

"Maybe I will have a glass of wine after all."

GRACE

Between the salad and the main course, I go to the powder room and call Sarah. She laughs and tells me that the baby comments were just a joke and she didn't realize it would be discussed at dinner. She also tells me to get off the phone, stop worrying about what others think, and enjoy myself.

The dinner is delicious and filled with great conversation. Not only is James attractive and polite, but he's also intelligent. Our dinner doesn't have moments of awkward silence or any awkward times. The conversation flows smoothly between us. We discuss our children, jobs, family, politics, and cancer-prevention techniques, which are basically to avoid smoking and to eat lots of fruits and veggies. We agree, however, that one major cause of cancer is bad luck. Even while discussing politics and illness, it didn't become uncomfortable or sad. For one thing, both of us vote the straight secret ballot, which means we didn't discuss politics. Also, we didn't really discuss illness; we mainly discussed how to avoid them.

I decide to ask him about the man he and Parker helped that night we were on the beach.

"Have you happened to hear anything about the man on the beach? The one you and Parker performed C.P.R. on?"

"I did. I called his wife to check on him and sadly, Walter didn't make it."

"Oh, I'm sorry to hear that."

"Thank you. Me, too."

"You know, sometimes God has other plans."

He nods his head in agreement. "You're right."

After dinner, James drives around Charlotte showing me some of the historical sights and he also drives past his medical office. Then he drives over to his condo where he lives. "I haven't been here in a few days, so would you mind if I run in and check on things?"

"No. Not at all. I know you've been vacationing on the island with Parker but when are you due to be back to work? Did you say, Monday?"

"That's right. I'll leave sometime tomorrow to return home. I know Parker and Sarah will be glad to have their home to themselves again."

"I'll miss seeing you around," I say honestly. It's been nice having him drop in randomly throughout the day.

"I'll be back, but I may need to find another place to stay while I'm there."

"I don't think you're a bother to Sarah or Parker when you're there."

"Maybe not, but they're young."

He drops the sentence there. He doesn't need to say anything else. I know what he means.

"There's a few vacation homes on the island but no hotels or condos."

"A house is too much for a single guy. I was thinking just a room with a kitchenette or something on the lines of that."

"Carly has her place above the bookstore. It's almost identical to my place and it's sitting empty."

He looks up at me. "She should be leasing that. It's in a good location and it'd be steady income. It's actually a great investment property and what she gets in rent may cover the mortgage on the building."

"She has it for rent but there's not much of an interest in it. Island life isn't for everyone. It's not like Daytona or Miami Beach where there's something always going on. Seashell Island is laid back and more exclusive."

"You have a point. Not exactly appealing to the younger crowd."

"Exactly."

Once we're inside his condo, he opens and reads the mail. His demeanor seems to change although he doesn't say anything. I watch as he lays a letter out flat and snaps a photo of it. It must be something important for him to want to take a picture of it. Then he waters the houseplants before feeding his beta fish, which he says is named Sandy Bottom Pants.

"You have a fish named Sandy Bottom Pants?" This is too funny. I can't be the only one who thinks this is hilarious. When I hear sandy, I think of sandy beaches, sandy toes, and land.

"You don't like her name?" he asks as he watches the fish swim around the small tank.

"I think it's a lovely name," I lie. "But how do you know it's a girl fish?"

"I don't know, but the purple color is pretty so I decided it must be a girl."

"Doctor logic?" I ask.

"At its finest." After a few minutes he says, "I need to make a private call. I'll be just a few minutes."

"Of course, take your time."

While standing at the kitchen bar, I wait for James while he goes into his bedroom to make the call. I look down at the opened letter that he took a photo of just a few moments ago. I scan the letter and when I read the word "complaint" I can't help but to scan the rest of it. I read the family of Walter Conrad is accusing Parker and James of possible negligence in the death of the 72-year-old man. I didn't get to read it word for word. I only had time to scan it. This is the man they helped on the island. The same man who was having the heart attack. We were just talking about this at dinner. He told me the man didn't survive. Certainly, the family can't think that James and Parker had anything to do with his demise. Neither of them had to help him at all, yet I can't imagine that either of them would have turned and walked away. Is this a lawsuit? Wouldn't a lawsuit notification come by certified mail? It mentioned a complaint was filed. I want to read this more thoroughly, but it would be an invasion of James' privacy. Since Parker is also involved, this could also affect Sarah. She can't know about this. If James just got a notice, maybe Parker also got a notice today, too. I want to call and ask or to give them a fair warning of what to expect. Maybe that's what James is doing now. I don't know James well enough to mention this to him, but how can I can continue this date knowing this is weighing heavily on his mind?

When he exits the bedroom, I don't hear him. I'm staring at the letter and my mind is on how someone can blame a person who did everything they could to save their loved one's life. Do they honestly believe Parker or James didn't do everything they could for him? I saw what they did for Walter. I was there offering comfort to the man's wife, Clara.

"I didn't want you to see that."

I look up with sadness prevalent on my face. "I'm sorry. I didn't mean to read it."

"It's okay."

"Does Parker know?"

"I just called him since he was named in the letter."

"Are you both being sued?"

"Do you want to sit down?" I walk away from the kitchen bar to the plush chair in the living area. He follows. "No, we aren't being sued. Medical professionals are protected by a Good Samaritan Law." I look up and watch him. "It's a law that protects medical professionals when they're off duty and try to help someone in need."

"Like in a car accident or someone having a heart attack?"

"Exactly. Medical professionals want to help, but we don't always have the equipment we need to perform life-saving techniques. And sometimes after we help, the person still dies."

"There's been enough lawsuits filed that there needed to be a Good Samaritan Law to protect the medical professionals from being sued needlessly?"

"Sadly, yes."

"I'm sorry."

"It comes with the job. I knew it going in as did Parker."

"It doesn't make it right," I say.

"No, it doesn't."

"You and Parker really do have a thankless job, don't you?"

"Sometimes we do, but so do law enforcement officers, power linemen, and several other professionals."

"Power linemen?" I ask, "I understand about law enforcement."

"Yes, power linemen. Every time a storm knocks out power, who do you think people blame?"

I may have been guilty of this a time or two. Going back to the letter sitting on the counter, I say, "So, if you're not being sued, then what's the letter about?"

"To inform us that a complaint was filed, and that the family of Walter Conrad isn't happy."

"I'm sorry. His wife is probably grieving and needed someone to blame."

He says, "I imagine one of their children filed the complaint."

"We were the only ones there?"

"We were. But they have three grown children. I'm sure one of them filed on the family's behalf." James stands and brushes his slacks off with his hands. "Let's not let this ruin our date. There's more I have planned for us this evening. Shall we?" he asks as he offers me his hand.

I take it and stand with him and smile. "I'm eager to continue," I say honestly.

"Good. Me, too."

Before leaving, James turns around and stuffs the letter in his jacket pocket before telling Sandy Bottom Pants goodbye.

JAMES

The rest of the date isn't as exciting as the first part. I never should have stopped by the condo. Although the Good Samaritan Law protects people like Parker and me, it's still tough to take when people aren't happy with our life-saving efforts when we're off duty. I would love to sit down with Walter's family and talk to them but it's not allowed. Once a complaint is filed, we're not allowed to have any contact with the family. But in Walter's case, he was alive when he left us in the ambulance.

On the drive back to the island, Grace and I stop for ice cream at a nearby ice cream parlor.

"I was hoping this date would have ended better than it did."

Grace laughs as she takes a bite of her mint chocolate chip ice cream. "I thought the date was wonderful."

"You do?"

"Yes. I don't have much to compare it with, but yes, I had a lovely time."

"Thank you. I think."

She giggles. "You still want to do some line dancing and karaoke singing next week?"

"Yes, I'd like to do something a little less formal and more fun."

"Good, so would I."

When I walk Grace up to her apartment, I stand at the door and wait for her to unlock it. I don't have any intentions of walking in. It's getting late and I need to return to Charlotte tomorrow and I also need to get ready to start back to work on Monday. I've been away for only a week, but a lot can happen in five days.

"Do you want to come in for a nightcap? I have cognac, wine, and beer."

My intention a minute ago was to go to Sarah and Parker's house, but how can a man deny an invitation to spend more time with a lovely woman. "I'd love one."

"I was hoping you'd stay a while longer."

That is music to my ears. She has a glass of wine and I decide on something stronger. A brandy is just what I need. There's no talk of lawsuits or death. We talk about life and how amazing it is to be healthy and able to enjoy it. We talk about the simple things in life like beach driftwood, seashells, and sea glass. We laugh at stories about her children, the amazing only church on the island, and about what wonderful parents she has.

She tells me about making homemade ice cream on the front porch of her family's vacation home. The home that her parents now live in full time.

I'm thankful that she didn't take long to open up about her life. The more she shares, the more I want to know about her. I think about how Parker is now a part of such a rounded family.

"My grandchildren will have an amazing life," I say before realizing I said it loudly.

"Grandchildren?" she says, watching me closely. "Do you know something that I don't know?"

"No, I swear. I just meant that whenever Parker and Sarah get married and have children, that their children will also have the same amazing life Sarah and Carly did growing up."

She watches me suspiciously. "I'm not sure I believe you entirely, James Taylor."

"I would never lie to you, Grace Stewart. If she's with child, I'm sure I'd be the last person they would tell."

"You and me," she says more calmly. "Just to be clear, I'm not opposed to them having children, but not just yet. A wedding would be nice, first."

She stands inside her apartment holding open the screen door as I stand on the porch. I really enjoyed myself this evening and I want to make sure the date for next weekend is secured.

"So we're still on for next Saturday, right?"

"Line dancing, karaoke, country music, who could pass that up?"

"Good. I'll pick you up at let's say six on Saturday?"

"Are you sure you want to drive to the island to get me, just to turn around and bring me right back a few hours later? Seems like a lot of driving in a single day for a date."

I look her from one eye to the other. "If it allows me to spend time with you, I don't mind the drive back and forth."

"How about I drive to Charlotte and meet you at your place on Saturday?"

I'm not sure I like this idea. With her driving herself, this means I'll miss out on the one-hour drive with her to and from Charlotte. I like the time we share together in the car. It gives us time to talk and get to know each other. "Can I get back to you on that?"

She laughs. "You can. Let me give you my business card so you have my number."

Do I dare tell her I already got her number from Sarah? I decide to not mention that. That's on a need-to-know basis and she doesn't need to know that.

Once she gives me her card, I tuck it safely into my wallet. I also give her my business card so she has my number in case she needs to call me for anything.

"Well, Grace. I had a great time with you this evening."

"I had a great time with you, too, James, and I'm looking forward to next week as well."

This brings a smile to my face. "So am I. I'll call you this week to confirm the details for Saturday."

"Sounds good. If I don't answer, leave a message and I'll be sure to return your call."

"I'll do just that." I wasn't going to kiss her, but how I can I deny myself the pleasure of her soft, sweet lips on mine. I take a step toward her. Slowly and cautiously. "May I kiss you?"

"I would like that," she says barely above a whisper.

My eyes fall from hers to her plump, soft, pink lips. I move slowly and cautiously as I close the distance to her mouth. My hands cup the nape of her neck holding her near. Once I feel her warm breath, I stop. I want to make sure she wants this as much as I do. Then our lips touch. She closes the distance between us. It's a closed-mouth soft kiss. It's not hot and passionate, but soft and sweet with a little heat. It feels like we both pull away at the same time.

She lightly touches her lips. "Well, that was nice."

"It was." I look behind her into her apartment. "Lock up and we'll talk later in the week."

"Okay, James. Thank you again for such a wonderful evening."

"Thank you, Grace. I'm looking forward to next Saturday."

"So am I."

***

The next morning Parker, Sarah, and I go out for breakfast before they go to church and I head home. We discuss the complaint from Walter Conrad's family that we didn't do enough to save their father and husband.

I show them the physical letter I got in the mail and tell Parker I'm sure he'll be getting one in the mail soon. He also knows that we are both covered under the Good Samaritan law where medical professionals are protected from lawsuits concerning off-duty emergency medical treatments. Sarah seems more upset than Parker and I are.

"You mean if you weren't covered under the Good Samaritan law they could sue you and you could lose your medical license, home, and everything you own?"

"Yes, that's right," I say. "But we are covered and it's fine."

"But what pisses me off is that they didn't appreciate what you both did do for Walter or for his wife." The bell over the door chimes, alerting us someone is coming into the small diner. I see the look on Sarah's face change, and Parker and I immediately look over. It's Walter's widow, Clara, and a man who's much younger. Maybe her son, Sam. I know right away Parker and I should leave. Sarah watches as they take a seat near the window. The man has never seen Parker and me, and Clara is in no condition to remember us. She was focused only on her husband's well-being. She now looks grief stricken. I wave for the waitress to get the check when I see Sarah stand from the table. Parker looks over at me, mouth wide open. Her shoulders and back are straight and her blonde ponytail and hips are swinging back and forth as she marches over to Clara's table. Parker and I stand from the table and watch. The orders are very simple when a complaint is filed with a Good Samaritan law. "Stay away from the families filing the complaint."

"Oh, this isn't going to be good," Parker says. "Sarah's been upset over this ever since you called last night. She can't understand the lack of respect Clara had for us and for what we tried to do for her husband."

"I don't think it was Clara who filed the complaint."

"I also questioned that."

Sarah maintains her voice in a low tone. Clara looks shocked, but the man with her looks angry. It confirms that Clara wasn't aware of the complaint filed against Parker and me. Now Clara seems to be reprimanding the man with her. Clara wipes away a tear and looks back at us. We remain standing. Now Sarah continues to speak. I decide it's time to save the man from Sarah's wrath.

We walk over together and Sarah doesn't stop talking. I should cut her off, but I listen instead. What she's saying is accurate and something I would say if I were allowed to speak to them.

"I was there. I saw what they did for your father. Your mother was frantic and your father was lying there. Unconscious, I might add. Doctor Blake and Doctor Taylor did everything they could for Walter and *we* are so very sorry for his untimely death." Sarah wipes away a tear before continuing. "But did you ever stop to think what would have happened if they chose to not stop to help your parents?" She waits for a response and the man just sits there. "Because they didn't have to do anything. They could have kept walking, offering no help to either of them." She pauses to catch her breath. I should stop her, but she's doing such a great job that Parker and I allow her to finish. "I saw your father. I saw what my boyfriend and his dad did for him *and* for your mother. Walter was alive when he left in the ambulance and this is the thanks they get?" Her face is red from anger. "It's because of people like you that they even have a Good Samaritan law. You should be ashamed of yourself."

Sam says, "I didn't file the complaint, one of my sisters did." He looks at Parker then to me. "My father had two broken ribs from their negligence," Sam insists.

"Your father was given C.P.R. Sadly, when given correctly, ribs can fracture. They even asked your mom for permission before performing it. He was alive and breathing on his own when the ambulance arrived."

Parker takes Sarah's hand and pulls her away from their table. Clara looks up at me and Parker. "We should go," I say, walking away.

Clara says, "Doctors, I owe you both an apology. I never once blamed either of you for Walter's death and I had no idea that anyone filed a complaint either." She looks over and glares at her son, who remains quiet. "I was there. I know what you both did for Walter *and* for me and I want to thank you both."

"We're sorry that your husband didn't make it, Clara. We hope you and your family are coping okay," I say. I try to keep the conversation cordial.

"Thank you."

The man still remains quiet.

Clara says, "We're actually here this weekend so we can clear our things out of the vacation home Walter and I were staying at while we were here the night… well you know."

I know she means the night he died. I look at Clara and then at Sam. "We need to get going," I say. "Again, we're very sorry for your loss."

Before we turn to leave, Clara says, "Sam and I will go down on Monday and rescind the complaint that was needlessly filed."

Sam says, "I'm sorry. Sarah explained to me what you both did for my father and mother. I didn't know that C.P.R. could result in rib fractures."

"Sometimes it can happen," Parker says.

"I guess my sisters and I needed someone to blame for my father's death."

"Again, we're sorry for your loss." Then we turn and walk away.

Once we're outside, Parker asks, "What all did you say to them?"

Sarah says, "She didn't know?"

"No. I guess not."

"I'm sure her children were grief—" I begin to say.

"I don't care what they were," she says loudly as her anger grows. "You don't do that to people who help you and you don't do that to *my* family."

I've never seen this feisty side of Sarah. I want to laugh, but I'm a little scared of her wrath.

Parker looks at his watch and says, "If we don't leave now, we'll be late for church. And Sarah, God knows that you need Jesus right now."

She hits him on his arm and laughs. "Was I too harsh?"

"No, babe. You were amazing."

"Well, we better hurry so we're not late for service."

Sarah looks at me in surprise. "You're coming with us?" she asks with a smile.

I'm not sure when I decided to stay longer on the island and go to church. My original plan was to go right home after breakfast. Is it to see Grace a little longer or is it after our run-in with Clara and Sam that I think some time closer to God is a good idea?

I know she thinks I'm staying for church service because of her mom, and maybe I am. "I think we can all use a little Jesus in our lives."

CHAPTER 4

JAMES

I use my drive home to Charlotte to think back on my time spent on the island.

After church and the potluck luncheon, I leave immediately for home. My mood is a better one and I can't say if it's from seeing Grace or hearing the gospel that Beau and Sarah's grandfather preached or receiving the sincere apology from Clara and her son. It could be a combination of everything. It could also be from the delicious meal we ate at the church right after the service. Seeing Grace sitting in the front pew holding her sleeping granddaughter surely warmed my heart. When Grace saw me in the church walking up to her, the smile and surprise on her face warmed the rest of my soul. She scooted over to make room for me to sit beside her. And then when she stood to sing with the choir she sounded like an angel.

I've had a great time with Parker and Sarah, but I also had a great time with Grace. It's easy to see why Parker fell so hard for Sarah. All of the Stewart women are amazing, beautiful, and down to earth. When I said my grandchildren would be lucky to be born into this amazing family, I wasn't kidding.

Once I'm in Charlotte, I decide to stop by the office first. I've been in touch with my office manager throughout the week and she's kept me informed of what's been going on. I know I have a busy workweek ahead of me, and I want to be prepared for it.

I walk in and lock up behind me. While walking around the empty office, I remind myself to give my office manager, Julie, a raise. The place looks amazing and clean. I sit in my office and go through the stack of charts of patients I'll see tomorrow. It'll be a busy day. There's a knock outside the building door, but I ignore it. We're closed. Whoever and whatever it is can wait until tomorrow. When the knock grows louder and harder, I decide to answer it. I'm surprised to see one of my employees standing at the back door.

"Anna?" I say, opening the door for her.

"I saw your car and thought I'd stop."

"Is something wrong?" I ask. Ever since she filed the sexual harassment complaint against Matt, my eyes have been opened to the risks we all could face. I just wish Matt would have talked to me about it, instead of just leaving. Parker said he thought it was a sign of guilt but I disagree. I can see why he wouldn't want to be involved in a scandal. Especially with what's going on in Hollywood. I'm not sure what to believe and what not to believe. He said, she said it's a tough argument to win.

"I need to speak with you," she says still standing outside of the office. I haven't invited her in yet. Now I wish I had a witness in the building. Just in case she ever accused me of anything.

"Okay." I lock up the door after her to keep anyone else from walking in. "We can talk here since no one else is here." Should I have divulged that information to her? Too late now.

She stops further inside the room and says, "I tried to call Julie, but she's not answering."

"She's probably busy. What can I help you with?"

"I need to take some time off this week. I'm still having those dizzy spells I told you about."

I didn't notice any vertigo when she walked in here. I motion with my hands to the chairs sitting nearest the doorway. "Sit down." Once we are both seated, I ask, "Did you see the doctor I referred you to?"

"I did. He ran some tests on me, but they all came back normal."

"Did you file the Family Medical Leave Act paperwork that Julie talked to you about?"

"No, not yet," she stammers.

"You'll need to do that."

"I just need a few days off." Now she sounds irritated.

"And you'll get them, but F.M.L.A. will also help ensure that you'll always get your days off. When you're out sick, it leaves the office staff short."

"I don't see what difference it makes if I have F.M.L.A. or not. I'm still sick no matter what."

I decide to not argue with her. "How long will you be out?"

"Maybe until Wednesday."

I raise a brow. That's not much of an answer. "You'll call as soon as you can if it'll be longer than that, right?"

"I will. I'm doing the best I can and I really am sorry."

I like Anna and I hope she's able to get better soon. At one time she was one of my best employees. But these last few months something's happened. She complains of dizziness although there's no medical evidence to explain why she would be dizzy. She takes time she doesn't have off work. I'm not saying she's making it up, but she's been off her game and it's affecting everyone who works with her.

"While you're out sick, fill out the F.M.L.A. paperwork and bring it back in with you when you return, and also bring in a doctor's slip from your physician."

"What? You don't believe me?"

"No. It's not that. I want to make sure you're taking care of yourself." I stand and walk to the door. "Is there anything else?"

She stands without difficulty. "No."

I wonder whether I should let her drive, but she leaves and walks out the door and down the street without showing obvious signs of vertigo. I close the door, call Julie, and leave her a message that Anna won't be in until later this week before getting back to reviewing my patients' files. Before I finish with the last person's chart, there's another knock at the door. Deciding it must be Anna, I stand to answer it. I'm thankful when it's Julie.

"Why didn't you use your key?" I ask, opening the door for her.

"I was out running errands and got your message so I decided to stop to talk to you. So, how was your vacation?"

Walking back to my office, I say over my shoulder, "Great. If you ever get a chance, you need to visit Seashell Island."

"From what you've said about it, I need some place with more action, more activity."

"Too laid back for you, is it?"

"Yeah, I think so." I sit down at my desk and she takes a seat across from me. "I got your message about Anna taking a few days off this week."

"She stopped in and said she's still not feeling well." Julie shifts in her seat. I look at the expression on her face. "You think there's more to it?"

"She was late for work almost every day last week. No excuses. No apologies."

"That's odd for her."

"Her behavior's been strange for a while. I'm not the only one who's noticed it. Others in the office have also said something about it. As the office manager I tried talking to her, but it didn't do any good. She became defensive like I was attacking her."

"All this started about the same time as the incident with Matt."

"I like Matt," she admits. "Although we joked and laughed a lot in the office, I never saw anything inappropriate from him. Ever."

Matt is recently married with a child. He's madly in love and happy. Anna's attractive, but I've never seen Matt do anything inappropriate either.

"It's unfortunate."

"Do you know where he is?" Julie asks. "I've called him, but he's changed his number."

I move the stack of files over to one side of my desk and stand. "No. I have no idea where he is or who he's working for. No one has called here for a reference on his employment."

Julie also stands. "I guess he doesn't want to be found."

"I guess not."

Nothing is spoken about who we believe or not. It's useless. Back to Anna and her tardiness. "Thank you for coming in and talking to me about Anna. I'll take it from here."

"I just think you should know what's been going on."

"Other than that, everything was good?"

"Everything was great."

We walk outside and say our goodbyes. On the way home, I call my doctor friend to see if Anna called him for an appointment and I'm not surprised to learn she hasn't.

Something needs to be done, but what?

GRACE

On Monday, Carly and Sarah came over to help me shop online for something to wear. I had an idea of what I wanted, but I didn't want to buy something that might be too much. They seemed to know what to get. I also wanted a cowgirl hat, but both girls were pretty adamant against it. I guess they know best.

He called on Wednesday just as he said he would. He talked for a short time, and I told him I would feel better if I drove to Charlotte on Saturday. It seems foolish for him to drive here to pick me up just to turn around and drive back again. Not unless he was coming to the island for other reasons that he didn't mention. He was reluctant at first, but agreed it made more sense.

This week I was in a really good mood. Getting my life back has everything to do with it. Living with my parents after my husband's death wasn't really living. I was existing. Living again just feels amazing. I still miss Michael, but I didn't die with him that dreadful day. The simple things of every day like seeing the smile on my parents' faces, or my children's and grandchildren's faces fills my heart. The breeze of the island air, shopping for fresh fruit, and walking along the beach's shoreline brings pleasure to my life. Spending time with James or the thought of spending time with him also makes me happy.

With every day that passes, I feel more like myself. I walk after work, read before bed, and do some yoga and meditation every morning to start my day. I also visit with Mom and Dad every evening and tell them how grateful I am for everything they've done for me and the girls over the years.

When I close up the shop on Saturday, I shower and call James before I leave for Charlotte. I want to make sure he hasn't changed his mind about me coming up.

"Hi, Grace," he answers cheerfully.

"Hi, James."

"You're not calling me to tell me you're having second thoughts, are you?"

"No. I'm heading out now. I'm just calling to see if you need anything."

"Not that I can think of. I thought we could have dinner here at home if that's okay with you before heading out for the night."

"Can you cook?" I ask, locking the apartment door behind me.

"Do you doubt my culinary skills?" I think I can hear laughter in his voice.

"Parker's said many good things about you, but being a culinary expert wasn't one of them."

"Oh, that's painful," he teases.

"Well, I could always be my own judge. After all, an opinion is subjective."

"You do make a very good point, Miss Grace." His tone turns serious. "In all seriousness, be careful on the drive here and call me if you run into any problems or need directions."

I unlock my car door using my key fob. "Okay, I will and I should be there in about an hour or so, depending on traffic."

"Traffic being the key word. It's Saturday in Charlotte. How bad can it be?" he teases.

"That's what I was afraid of. Did I mention how much I enjoy living on the island?" I ask before pulling out onto Shell Lane.

"You mean because you can walk from one end to the other in less than an hour?"

I laugh. It's true, you can do that. "That and other things."

"You may have mentioned that a time or two."

"Just making sure. But I'm leaving now and I'll see you in about an hour." I hope.

"Great, while you're driving I'll be slaving away at a culinary masterpiece."

"I'll be the judge of that."

We both laugh and say our goodbyes. I then decide to listen to country music on my way to Charlotte.

I haven't felt butterflies like these in my belly since… the last time I saw James and then the only times before that was when I'd see my husband. I pull into the parking spot beside James' car and take some deep breaths to try to get my breathing under control. Before I can get out of the car, James is already walking towards me. He's wearing Levi jeans, a plaid shirt, and cowboy boots. He doesn't look like the professional doctor that he looked like last week. I have to admit I liked the suit-and-tie look but this cow-wrangler look he's sporting today is undeniably sexy in a totally different way. I can't help but smile as he makes his way to my car.

I open the door and step out. "Howdy," I say in my best country accent. I'm also wearing Levis, a plaid shirt, and boots. Sarah also insisted on getting me a belt with an overly large belt buckle. I never understood why until now. His eyes fall from my eyes to the buckle. I cough and he looks up at me.

He laughs when he realizes he was caught ogling my… buckle. "I didn't mean to stare but does that buckle say something or is it strictly there for looks?"

The wind blows and I get a whiff of his signature scent of spice, sandalwood, and musk.

My heart races when I realize Sarah wanted James to see other parts of me and not just my face. "I'm going to kill your future daughter-in-law."

"I see." He laughs and then smiles. He takes my hand and walks me into his condo. "Have I told you how I much I like Sarah?"

I bet he does. "You know she was a handful as a child, too, right?"

"I can only imagine." He looks down at me. "You look beautiful by the way."

I want to look away but I hold his stare. He always says the nicest things. "Thank you."

Once inside his condo, I have a glass of wine and he has a Scotch on the rocks. "I thought we could Uber tonight," he says as an explanation for his drinking.

"I've never actually taken an Uber before."

"Really?"

"We don't have them on the island."

He laughs as he stirs the pot of pasta. "I keep forgetting that. The island's so small you can toss a stone from one end to the other."

"That's not true." I cross my arms over my chest.

"Are you sure?" he teases. "Have you ever tried?"

I take a sip of my wine. "The island is nearly two miles wide, and I'm pretty sure no man *or* woman has ever tossed or thrown a rock the distance of two miles."

"Wow, two miles wide." He laughs again and I realize just how small our precious island is. "That big, is it?"

"On second thought, maybe someone has kicked a rock that far down the road."

He lowers the temperature on the pasta and joins me on the other side of the bar with his drink. "It is a pretty special place where you live. I'm glad that Parker's decided to make it his home."

"Me, too. Parker's been great for Sarah."

"They've been good for each other." There's a silence between us. "Have you thought about the songs you want to sing tonight?"

I'm pretty confident in my singing, but should I tell him that or should I let him believe I'm shy and timid? Shy and timid sounds like more fun. "I've been practicing a few songs. I didn't want to get up there and be completely lost."

"It can be intimidating for first timers. But you do sing in the choir so I think you'll be fine."

"Singing in a choir and singing in a bar. I'm pretty sure that's a huge difference."

He chuckles. "Yeah, you're right. Drunk people don't care how you sound."

He dishes up the plates of food and we discuss the songs over our meal. Just as I suspected, James is an excellent chef. I've always given credit when credit is due. Although he knows he can cook, he doesn't like compliments. He brushes it off as if he's cooked something from a box. I decide to leave it at that. He boasted about his culinary skills, but then he shied away from compliments. He's a very modest man. Sometimes.

After dinner and when everything is cleaned up, he gets on his cell phone and arranges for an Uber driver.

"How long will a driver take to get here?" I ask, expecting the answer to be a half an hour or longer.

"He's rounding the corner now." He picks up his keys and tucks them into his pocket.

I stand. "He's here? Now?"

"Yes. You thought it would take longer?"

"I did." I follow him to the door and walk out into the near darkness. The driver stays in the car while James holds the back door open for me. I get in and scoot over, and then he climbs in after me. The ride isn't an awkward one like I thought it would be. We talk like we're among friends including the driver into the conversation. I give James and the driver credit for that. Once we arrive at our destination, there's no money exchanged between James and the driver, just a friendly goodbye. When the driver's out of sight, I ask, "Did you pay him?"

"I did. It was all done on the app."

"And the tip?"

"Yep. That, too. I just added a tip and a review," he says, swiping a finger across his cell phone screen.

"I think I could get used to this car-service thing."

He takes my hand and loops it through his arm. "Come on, Grace. Let's dance."

***

Although it's early, the place is already getting busy. Once we get a seat and our drinks, James wastes no time hitting the dance floor. He's more relaxed this week than he was last week. I guess anyone would be in jeans and a flannel shirt. I shouldn't be surprised he's an excellent dancer, too. I'm starting to wonder if there's anything this man isn't good at. While he knows every line dance there is, I sit out on the ones I don't know. It gives me a chance to admire him from a distance. It makes me smile when I see other women attempt to flirt with him and how he's friendly but politely ignores their advances.

During the next hour we sit outside on the patio where it's cooler and enjoy each other's company. "Are you having a good time, Grace?"

"I am. I hope I'm not embarrassing you too much."

His eyes get big. "Embarrassing me, how?"

While sitting on the bar stool, I hold out both of my legs. "You know, with my two left feet."

"You have nothing to worry about. You're an amazing dancer." He looks at his watch and says, "It's almost time for karaoke. Do you want to go there now or would you rather stay here for a bit longer?"

"Oh, no. We're going. I've been exercising my vocals all week for this." I offer a playful grin.

"Who am I to argue with the pretty lady?" He gets on his phone and summons an Uber driver. "Ready?"

"I really need to get one of those things," I say, referring to the Uber app. I like the thought of pushing a button and having a driver available within a few minutes.

JAMES

While in the Uber car, I download the app and info into Grace's phone that she'll need if she ever gets the opportunity to use an Uber. "Now you can also have a car at your beck and call."

She laughs. "Assuming one's available in my area."

"That's the catch."

I offer for the driver to come back when he gets off work. I even tell him I'll buy him a drink later. To my surprise he rejects my offer with an explanation that he has a better offer with a girl he drove earlier. I have no idea if this is allowed, but who am I to stand in the way of a man and a pretty woman.

Once inside the bar, I get us drinks and a table. Grace excitedly searches the karaoke book for songs for us to sing. The bar is full and this doesn't surprise me. Every time I'm here, it's busy. Grace asks before she writes down any songs on the list. I agree to all of them, but I secretly question one of them. The artists are legends and if you mess up the audience usually isn't very forgiving, unless the bar is full of happy drunks. I also have a few songs I want to add to the list. I doubt we'll have time to get through all the songs, but I've never had anyone to sing with and I plan to take full advantage of it. I watch as Grace hands the list of songs to the DJ. She doesn't look nervous, but more excited.

They don't call our names first. I always feel sorry for the person whose name they do call first. Not that they ever get booed, but what if they did? It would be the end of my amateur singing career. Grace laughs a lot and is having a great time.

When they call our names, I can see fear in her eyes. I take her hand and offer her my best cowboy smile. She smiles back but fear quickly appears. "What if they hate me?"

"You have nothing to worry about. If we get booed, it'll be because of me. Not you."

"You don't think that'll happen, do you? I'll die if that happens."

I want to laugh but then I feel bad when I see panic set in. "No, Grace. I was just teasing."

I take her hand and gently urge her onto the stage. I see several familiar faces. I let Grace decide which song to start with. She leans in and whispers to the D.J. I hand her a mic before taking one for myself. Then I wait for the music to start so I can prepare for the song. I'm surprised she chose "Remind Me" by Brad Paisley and Carrie Underwood for the first song. Grace looks at me and she looks more relaxed. I guess music also calms her. She's tapping her foot to the music, so I do the same. She smiles brightly when I have to go first. Lucky for her, I like this song and lucky for me, I know it. We have fun and I soon realize she's a natural with a mic and in front of a crowd. I knew she could sing from listening to her in the choir at the church but I had no idea that gospel voice was just as amazing while singing country. She probably sounds amazing singing in the shower, too. I'd like to find out. At the end of the song she gets a standing ovation. I say she because I sing here all the time and I've never had everyone in the entire room stop and applaud for me before. She smiles and hugs me tightly. I think I like the hug more than the ovation.

I also applaud her and she smacks my arm. "Stop it. This is for us."

"No, honey. This is *all* for you," I say, waving my hand around the room at the crowd.

We hug again and before we walk off the stage someone yells, "More!"

I know it's not our turn since I saw the many names on the sign-up list when the D.J. handed me the mics. The D.J. yells, "What song will it be?"

Grace looks at me. "Your choice."

I ask the D.J, "How about Kid Rock and Sheryl Crow's 'Picture'?"

"Sounds good to me," he says, searching for the song.

That song also ends in a standing ovation. We end the night with "Islands in the Stream" by Kenny Rogers and Dolly Parton. This is the song I was worried about messing up. Kenny and Dolly are both country icons and their music's loved by millions maybe even billions. Music lovers sometimes don't like when others attempt to sing their songs and fail to reach the proper notes or tunes. We've got a great crowd and I pray this song sounds just as amazing as the others we already sang tonight.

Dolly is one of the greatest country singer-songwriters ever, but lots of children know her as the lady who gives them books. She does this because her father was illiterate despite being a brilliant man. A very young child whose family joins Dolly's online Imagination Library program receives a free age-appropriate book each month from birth until the child starts school. Dolly started the program in 1995, and by the middle of February 2018 it had sent out over 100 million free books. I'd call her "Saint Dolly," but she prefers The Book Lady or just Dolly." Her father lived long enough to hear children call her The Book Lady.

At the end of the song and yet another standing ovation, I decide it's time to make our exit. I was nearly afraid people would surround Grace and ask for her autograph or worse, ask her for her phone number.

"I can't tell you the last time I had so much fun," she says, nearly breathless, as she climbs into the Uber car.

Her smile tells me this night will be one she'll remember for a long time to come. "Me, either," I say honestly.

"Really?" She wipes the sweat from her brow.

I ask the driver to make a pit stop at the closest gas station so I can get Grace some water.

He says, "I have some in the trunk; it's warm, but you're more than welcome to it."

"I'll take it. Thank you." When he gets out of the car to get the water, I turn to Grace. "I had an amazing time."

"But you do this all the time."

"I do, but you've never been with me before."

"Aww, James. That's so sweet. Thank you."

"The crowd loved you." It's true.

"And you."

The driver gets in and hands us each a bottle of Dasani water. I'll make sure to compensate him for his kindness. I've been offered mints and water before from drivers but never Dasani brand. Of course, I know this is from his personal stash.

"Are you hungry? Do you want to stop someplace for a sandwich, dessert, or a nightcap?" I look at my watch and it's getting late. I hate to think of her driving home tonight.

"Sure. I'd love to continue to hang out with you a little longer."

"Good."

"Can we go someplace a little quieter?"

"Do you want to go back to the condo or we could go someplace more public? I swear no matter where we go I'll be a gentleman."

"I'm not worried about that. Your condo's fine."

When we get back to the condo, one laugh, one look, one kiss, one thing led to another. We both had been drinking, but we weren't drunk by any means. The passion. The spark was fast and furious. I've never experienced anything so explosive before in my life.

I don't think either of us expected this, at least I know I didn't, and I'm pretty sure Grace didn't either. The love making started in the living room and ended in the bedroom. I swore I'd be a gentleman, and gentlemen sometimes make love.

In the morning I lie in bed and watch her sleep. My mind replays her smell, her touch, and her moans in a vivid slow motion. My dick thickens at the thought. The way her body moved in sync with mine. The way she let her needs be known. This night will be one I will never forget. I want more. I need more. She's intoxicating.

I just pray she doesn't wake up with regrets. What if everything was a result of the euphoria we felt from the night at the club. It was pretty spectacular, even for me. God. Maybe I should have stopped it. No. She wanted it. She wanted it just as much as I did. We both wanted it and God knows that I needed it. She makes me feel alive and with purpose.

She wakes up and smiles at me. "Good morning, James."

"Good morning, beautiful. Did I wake you?"

She rolls over on her side and reaches her hand out for mine. "No, I wasn't asleep."

"You weren't?"

"No, I was reliving the incredible night we shared." She scoots closer to me.

"It was pretty extraordinary."

"That it was." I tuck her small frame close to my body and she begins to slowly kiss my chest. My dick quickly rises to the occasion.

She giggles as she presses her body against mine. "Just to be clear," she says. "Last night was totally out of character for me, but I don't regret one minute of any of it." Her voice is raspy and sexy.

"I'm glad. What happened between us was totally unexpected and incredible."

She slowly runs her nails down my side and back up my leg, just stopping at my waist. "Whew, it was amazing and everything happened in a rush of sexual desire of need and want." She pauses and says, "Well, that's how I remember it."

I roll her over on her back and hover over her. I lean in and kiss her as I have no words to say. Sexual desire of need and want about sums up the way I remember. She moans and the sound is all too familiar.

We stay in bed and I swear every time is like the first time. I can't get enough of her. She's insatiable. We don't get out of bed until sometime in the afternoon when her belly growls from hunger. She wears one of my dress shirts and it takes all I have to not take her again.

At her insistence, she makes us omelets for breakfast while I make the coffee. She maneuvers around the kitchen like she's been here a hundred times. I don't have a problem with her cooking while I sit back and admire her bare legs while envisioning her body beneath the white dress shirt that I've become very acquainted with over the last several hours. I'm beginning to wonder how I'll make it an entire week without seeing her.

I decide I can't take it anymore and walk over to assist my services. When I stand behind her at the stove, she laughs.

"James?" She giggles.

"Mmm hmm," I reply with my mouth to her ear.

"You better put that thing away." We both laugh. "At least until after we eat. I'm starving."

"Okay. I get that. I'll just busy myself over here somewhere," I say, walking over to the coffee pot. "But you have to know you can't wear something like that and not think it'll affect me."

"Thank you," she says as she stands on her tiptoes to turn over the omelet. I watch her hoping the shirt rises a little higher. I then tend to the coffee to take my mind off of the beauty standing in my kitchen.

We have a very late breakfast at the kitchen bar eating out of the pan she cooked the omelet in.

The breakfast is casual and it doesn't feel awkward in the least. Grace is carefree and happy and looks more relaxed than I've ever seen her. I'd like to think I have something to do with that.

When Grace leaves just after five pm, we have made plans for the upcoming weekend. I'll go to Seashell Island this time. We haven't spoken of seeing other people, but there isn't anyone else I would rather spend my time with. The more time I'm with her, the more amazing she is.

She calls me when she gets home. I don't ask her what she told her daughters or parents about not being in church this morning. I know that they know she was here with me. Parker hasn't called me bitching me out so maybe he's okay with this, too. A man can hope, right?

~~~

On Tuesday afternoon, Anna walks in just after lunch under the influence of drugs and/or alcohol. I guess she forgot that she requested time off. I had no choice but to fire her. I won't condone behavior like this. It's sad since once she was one of my most valued employees.

The next day near closing time, Julie walks into the office with a huge grin on her face. It's not the normal happy grin that says "it's closing time" — it's more of a mischievous grin like, I have a secret.

"What?"

"Did you have a good time over the weekend?" she asks, taking a seat across from my desk. She has her cell phone and car keys in her hand.

Sitting back in the chair, I smile at the memory. I had a great time but how could she know that? "I did. Thank you." Since this is a place of business and professionalism, I rarely share details of my personal life unless it has to do with my son. Even then, I share very little. So, this makes me wonder why she's asking about my weekend. "How was yours?"

"Not as good as yours," she says, laughing.

I don't recall seeing her or anyone else from the office out that night. It makes me wonder how she can be so certain. She presses a button on her cell phone and a familiar tune plays through her phone speaker. It's "Islands in the Stream," but it's not by the original recording artists. It's by Grace and me. A smile spreads across my face at the memory of Grace and I ending the night with a song that was a huge hit on Saturday. I may also be smiling at what happened at my place later.

"Where did you get that?"

"Have you been on YouTube lately?" Her smile is now spread across her face. She turns her phone around so I can see the amateur video someone posted on YouTube of Grace and me. It was recorded Saturday night when Grace and I were singing karaoke. My eyes get big as I watch Grace and I sing freely. "You're an overnight sensation. This video has several thousand hits."

"Let me see that." I take the phone to get a better look at the video. She's right. The video has been seen by many with several thumbs up. People are commenting about the hot new duo. I can't help but smile when I see how relaxed and carefree Grace is. She's gorgeous. I wonder whether she has seen this yet. Probably not. Her children will know about it before Grace will. I should call and let her know. When I hand the cell phone back to Julie, I ask, "I'd appreciate it if you'd keep this between us." Meaning please don't share it with the office staff.

"Yeah. About that."

"They already know?"

"Gemma showed it to me." That's when I hear the girls in the other room singing to the YouTube video and laughing about it. It's impossible not to laugh with them. I've always encouraged fun and laughter in the workplace, but not at my expense. I'll let them have fun at me this time. After all, it is pretty funny.

I stand and walk towards the door to leave. Julie follows. "Y'all seem to have a lot of free time on your hands," I say, walking through the waiting area to the front door, "I'll have to see if I can't find a way to increase your workload tomorrow." I hold the door open, and each staff member walks through still singing off key and laughing hysterically.

"Don't worry, Kenny," Gemma teases, "your secret is safe with us."

If I'm Kenny, I guess that makes Grace, Dolly. I think I might be okay with that. Smiling brightly, I say, "I can see that. Get on out of here." We all part ways and I find myself humming on the drive home.

Later that night when I call Grace to tell her, Sarah and Carly are at her apartment. They also saw the video and came over to playfully harass her about it. They're both signing loudly in the background. The singing becomes faint and Grace walks further away from her daughters.

"James, I had no idea we were being recorded."

"Me, either, but there were a lot of people there that night."

"There were. I want to tell you again how much fun I had."

It brings a smile to my face. "Me, too. I'm kind of glad someone recorded us."

She sounds surprised. "You are?"

"I am. It's one of our first dates and it's nice to have it on video. It'll give us something to look back on later and we can laugh about it."

"With or without the video, it was a night to remember and I don't think I could ever forget it."

And I think that is the nicest thing anyone has ever said to me. "Thank you. It was memorable, and now we'll never be able to forget it."

As if that night isn't already burned into my memory.

CHAPTER 5

GRACE

I hang up and let the girls continue with their joking. I know they've never seen me like that and it makes them happy to see me let go.

"Seriously, Mom. You were smokin'," Sarah says.

Carly agrees. "You did look great. I knew you could sing, but I've never heard you sing anything but gospel before."

"I like all sorts of music but next to gospel, country is my favorite."

"Oh, my, God. The videographer zoomed in on your belt buckle. I knew your wearing that was a good idea."

I look over at Sarah when I remember James looking at it. "The videographer wasn't the only one who noticed that buckle."

"I don't doubt that." Sarah pleasantly smiles. "And who knew James could carry a tune?" Sarah asks while looking on her phone at the YouTube video. "Look at all those views! You know what that means?"

"Yes, it means you've watched it a lot since you first learned it was posted."

"It means people are liking this video. Have you read the comments?"

"No, I haven't." I do plan on watching the video and reading some of the comments after they leave. I surely don't want to do it with them here. This is a bit embarrassing.

"Put your phones down and let's have dessert," I say, changing the direction of the conversation.

They do and we talk more seriously about James and me.

"It looks like you really like him," Carly says.

"I do like him and he's a lot of fun. What's not to like? But we've gone out only a couple times. It's nothing serious."

We've slept together. A lot. Does that make us serious? I know I have no interest in dating other people. I'm not sure how James feels about that. We didn't do much talking once we got to his place. I'm glad that Carly and Sarah aren't teasing me about staying with him that night. I told a little white lie about being too drunk to drive and how he graciously offered me his bed for the night. Okay, it was a huge lie and he offered me more than his bed.

Sarah asks before taking a bite of her chocolate cake, "Are you seeing him this weekend?"

"We may be having dinner this weekend."

"On the island?" Carly asks.

"Yes, he's coming here."

"You may have been out only a few times but you've spent a lot of time together."

"That's true, Carly, we have. But again, it's nothing serious. He's great to hang out with, and I like having someone to do things with."

"I'm glad it's working out. I think he's a great guy," Sarah says and Carly agrees.

"I do, too."

Once they leave, I open the laptop and watch the video in private. My cheeks hurt from smiling so much. The comments are sweet and hilarious. James has some marriage proposals from women, some comments are saying we're an amazing and talented couple, and some are commenting on my belt buckle, which makes me blush. We have some thumbs-down, but someone commented, "Oh, look. Some people were so busy pressing REPEAT that they accidentally pressed THUMBS-DOWN." The video has more views than before. I decide to do another search of James on YouTube. I also see he has a fan club he must not know about. I bookmark this page before shutting off my computer.

That night I dream of country music and dinner. I dream of fun and laughter. I dream of a handsome man with a magical voice. I dream of amazing sex. I dream of James.

The next few days I focus on work, making candles, and wreaths. It seems the candles and wreaths are the biggest sellers. Carly's books and Sarah's haiku postcards are also big sellers. I finally talked Sarah into collecting some of her poems in a booklet-sized paperback book. I'm excited to see them when they come in. The shop is busy, and I have to admit that it was exactly what I needed. I will never be able to thank Mom and Dad enough for giving me my life back. It couldn't have come at a better time. I'm not sure how they knew it was time, but they did. I'm excited when I see them stroll into the shop.

"I wasn't expecting to see you guys here today."

"It was too nice to stay home all day so we came out for lunch and thought we'd see how your shop was doing."

I look at Mom as she makes her way around my shop, sniffing a few candles as she goes.

"It's going well. I'll be making more candles later this evening along with a few more wreaths."

"You can make them at the house tonight if you want to," Mom suggests.

"Okay. I can do that. I'll come over right after work and then after dinner we can make crafts."

"It sounds good. I always like the way the house smells during and after you make your candles."

After I finish making candles, the scent lingers into the house for many days after.

I wonder if my mom misses me there with her. I have dinner with them on most evenings, but am I spending enough time with them? "I miss your help," I admit.

Mom looks up with a smile. "I miss helping you, too."

Dad stands near the register. "It always looks and smells so nice in here."

"Thank you, Dad."

"Are you happy, Grace?" he asks.

I offer my best smile. "I am."

Mom walks up and says, "Well, that's all that matters."

Dad says, "Grace, you look happy."

I can feel myself smiling for no reason. "I am, Dad."

He gives me a big hug and kisses my cheek. "Good. Is this because of Parker's father, James?"

He may have something to do with it. "Honestly, I think it's because I have my independence back. The shop is a huge help and it keeps me busy. People are in and out of the shop throughout the day, and most are very friendly and chatty. You and Mom knew what you were doing when you bought me the shop." I look at both of them. "I'll never be able to thank either of you enough."

Mom says, "We saw the girls moving on with their lives and as much as we loved having you there with us, we knew it was time. It was past time and we felt we were enabling you for so long after Michael's death. You spent so much time in mourning. We should have encouraged you to move on, get out, and meet people. But we were also torn with protecting you and giving you time to deal with your loss."

This is turning somber, and I never want my parents to feel bad for protecting me. They were a Godsend in my darkest days, and my darkest days turned into darkest months and years. Without them, I'm not sure what would have become of me, Carly, or Sarah. God knows I wasn't well enough to care for them on my own.

"Well, if you ask me, I think you chose a perfect time to turn me loose."

Mom smiles. "Really?"

"I do. It was time. My life here on the island with my parents, children, and grandchildren is nearly perfect. I'm doing what I love and I have a reason to smile again."

"That's all we needed to hear."

Once they leave the shop, I call Carly and Sarah and ask them if they want to all meet over at their Pap's and Gram's house for dinner. I encourage everyone to bring their swimsuits and we'll just spend an evening swimming in the heated pool, cooking, and making crafts. Parker suggests that we have a BBQ. I think this is just what Mom and Dad need. A night with the entire family.

The night ends later than I expected, but it was just what everyone needed. Mom played with baby Maria while everyone else swam with Myra. Beau's dad even came over for the evening. The only person who was missing was

James. I often thought about him and wondered what he was doing tonight. I knew Parker never had a family like this, and I've never heard or asked about James' parents. Are they close? Are they still alive? Are we the only family Parker has other than his father?

***

On Friday afternoon, James calls to see if I want to have a late dinner with him when he comes in town. I think about going over and eating with Mom and Dad and then having coffee or dessert with James. Then I get a better idea.

"Do you want to join me for dinner at my parents' house? I usually eat dinner with them throughout the week." When there's a pause, I think about how this may sound. He may think I'm asking him to meet my parents or something. Do older men fear this like younger men do or did? I decide to remind him he already knows them. "You met them at the Christmas Eve party and then again at church."

"I remember. How are they?"

"They're well. Thanks for asking."

"It's short notice. Do you think they'll mind having another person over for dinner?"

"No. Trust me, they'll love it."

"Okay, then. I'll call you when I leave the office then it'll take me nearly an hour to get there depending on traffic."

"Do you need an address or do you remember how to get there?"

"I think I can find it but send me the address just in case."

"Okay. I'll see you soon."

"I'm looking forward to it," he says before hanging up.

And there's those butterflies again.

***

After work, I stop at Tony's market and pick up some things for dinner. Dad thought steaks on the grill was a good idea and Mom and I agreed. James pulls in right around six o'clock and I meet him outside on the porch. To my surprise, he brought wine for everyone and flowers for my mom.

He embraces me in a hug and a kiss on the front porch. I eagerly return the kiss. It's not as passionate as last weekend but the fire and passion are still there.

"I've missed you," he says between kisses.

I touch his cheek with my hand. "I missed you, too."

James has changed out of his work clothes and into jeans and a black tee. Dad and James cook the steaks on the grill while Mom and I set the outside dinner table bringing the food out. She makes sure the centerpiece is the flowers James brought her.

Dinner is filled with polite conversation and laughter. I watch the interaction James has with my parents, and it's nice to see how well he fits into my world. No matter how short or long this lasts between us, I intend to enjoy every minute of it.

After dinner and when everything's cleaned up, we sit outside by the outdoor fireplace and have coffee and dessert. Mom and Dad are happy and relaxed. I watch the way Dad's doting on Mom: offering to get her a throw, refilling her coffee when it's nearly gone, holding her chair out for her when she stands or sits down. It's no wonder they've been together for so long.

This was the way Michael was with me and it's also the way James is. James holds my hand openly and smiles often. I watch as Dad takes notice of the way he treats his daughter.

"What are your plans for the weekend?" Dad asks James.

"I thought Grace and I could rent one of the pedal boats and spend the day on the water tomorrow."

Mom looks over at me. Tomorrow's Saturday and my shop's open for business on Saturday. It's one of my busiest days of the week. As much fun as that sounds like, I have work. I don't say anything. I'm not sure how to break the news to him.

Dad says, "Beauregard and Carly own a pedal boat. They rarely use it since baby Maria was born. You can grab lunch at Tony's market and you'll be set for the day." Dad looks at me and smiles. "What time should your mom and I be there to take over the shop?"

I can tell when James realizes that my business is open on Saturday. "We can do it later in the day. Toward evening?" he suggests politely. "Or Sunday after church?" He doesn't want to put my mom and dad out. He needs to return to Charlotte on Sunday and he usually leaves earlier in the day.

"Nonsense. It'll be too cold to be on the water at dusk. Larry and I can handle the shop just fine." Mom adjusts the blanket on her lap. "Besides, I've been wanting to get in there and see everything anyway. It's hard to shop when I'd rather visit with my daughter instead."

I know not to argue with Mom. I look at James. "Is noon okay?"

"Perfect."

"Thanks, Mom and Dad."

Dad smirks. "You may want to hold off on the thank you until you see how short your inventory is after Sylvia leaves."

Mom playfully hits Dad on the arm. "You'll pay for whatever I take."

"That's what I'm afraid of," he says, wrapping a secure arm over her shoulder.

"Thank you both," James says, "I need to be more informed the next time. We've gone out only in the evenings. I didn't consider the shop being open tomorrow."

"It's an easy fix," Dad says.

We visit for only a few more minutes before James and I leave. Once outside he apologizes again.

"Please, don't be sorry. I think it sounds like a wonderful day. I don't know the last time I was in a pedal boat."

"Good. I'll call Beau when I get home to make sure it's okay that we use his."

"I can call."

"Please, let me. I feel it's my manly duty to do the begging… I mean asking."

"Okay, do you have his number?"

"I can get it from Sarah and Parker." He adds, "I don't think I'm scoring any points with your family."

"Why is that?"

"I feel bad for your Mom and Dad having to cover for you at your shop tomorrow."

"It's okay. The shop closes early on Saturdays so Mom and Dad will need to be there only a few hours."

"You don't think they'll mind tending to the shop?"

"No, not at all. If they did care, they wouldn't have offered."

We hold hands as we make our way down the driveway, I ask, "Do you want to come over for a little while?"

"Are you sure?"

"It's still early. Not unless…" I begin to say. Maybe he had other plans. Maybe he wants to see his son.

"I'd love to."

"Good, I'll follow you there in my car."

James parks his car down from my apartment at Parker's medical practice. I'm not sure if it's because he doesn't want people on the island knowing we're seeing each other or what. It's probably a good idea. People on the island will surely find it news worthy if his car was parked next to mine after hours of my shop being closed.

He holds my hand as we walk up the stairs to my apartment. "You look beautiful tonight."

I decided to wear a flowing red and white dress with red strappy heels. I would have been more comfortable in jeans and a sweater, but I wasn't sure what he'd be wearing.

"Thanks. Would you like coffee or wine? I also have some brandy and beer if you'd like something else."

"Are you up to a fire on the beach?" Before I can answer, he says, "I'm sure we can find some driftwood. We can take a bottle of wine and things over to make s'mores."

I've never done that before. I've been to beach parties with several dozen people and a huge bonfire. But just me and another person, would be new to me. "Yeah. That sounds like fun."

"I was hoping you would say that. I was also wondering what you told your family about last weekend."

My heart rate picks up at the memory. "I told them the truth."

His eyes get big and he stutters, "What part of the truth did you tell them exactly?"

"That I got drunk and that you graciously offered me your bed."

He pulls me into a tight hug and kisses me. "So, you told them a version of the truth. You weren't drunk and I did offer you my bed."

"It was amazing," I whisper at the memory.

"That it was, Grace."

He kisses me again and I suddenly want to stay in and have a repeat of last weekend.

"You better change before it's too late."

I pull away slowly. I know he's right. "I'll just be a minute."

CHAPTER 6
JAMES

Every time I find a piece of driftwood to burn, Grace wants to keep it for a decoration or for one of her craft projects.

"If you insist on keeping every piece of driftwood, we won't have anything to build a fire with."

"I know." She laughs. "But every piece is so unique."

Finally, I tell her to search for the driftwood while I go into Tony's market and buy some precut firewood. Thankfully, he has some for sale.

Once the fire is built, we sit on the quilt in front of the fire watching the waves slap along the shoreline. She attempts to roast the marshmallows, but I soon realize she has no patience. "They're called roasted marshmallows, not burnt marshmallows."

She laughs, revealing a youthful smile despite her age. "I should have told you earlier that I can't cook marshmallows over an open fire, or in the oven with sweet potatoes."

"Wait a minute. Are you telling me you can't cook?" I remember vividly the omelet she made us last weekend.

"Is that a deal breaker for you?" she teases.

I can see the humor in her eyes. She can burn water and that won't dissuade me in any way. "No, not at all. I'm just asking."

"Not to brag or anything, but I'm actually a pretty good cook as you may remember."

"I remember that very well." My dick twitches when I realize I need to talk about something else. Last weekend was amazing. We were in the privacy of my home, but this weekend we're here on the island and I'm pretty sure Grace will want certain things about us kept between us. At least for now. I take the stick from her and apply another marshmallow. "Here, I'll *roast* them, and you can make the s'mores when they're done."

"Now that's something I can handle."

We make s'mores and cuddle. We kiss and she snuggles into me. We kiss some more and it's nice. It's romantic and it feels good to be with her. We're near the fire, under the stars and moon, with the rolling waves in the background crashing onto the beach. This night wasn't planned, but it's damn near perfect. Just as last weekend wasn't planned either. I like the feel of her lips on mine. I like the smell of her scent wafting in the air. I like the feel of her skin against mine.

We drink a bottle of wine and watch as the fire dwindles down to just hot embers. "We're out of firewood unless you want to part with some of your driftwood?" I whisper into her ear.

She giggles. "Looks like we better head home." I didn't think she would part with her precious driftwood. We both stand and I kick some sand to extinguish the hot embers. After folding the blanket, we gather the trash and the driftwood, and then I take Grace's hand and walk with her across the street to her apartment.

"We haven't discussed about you staying with me tonight."

I look over at her. "I know. It's a bit different this week."

"It is. I'd like for you to stay."

I think about her children and parents and what people would think and say. Not about me but about her. Then I decide me staying the night with her is a bad idea. It's a small island and gossip, good or bad, would travel quickly. I would never put her in a situation where her reputation could be tarnished. I decide to let her make the decision.

"Do you think that's a good idea?"

We cross the street to her apartment and she's quiet for a few seconds as if she thinking.

"Probably not. It's a small island."

"It is," I agree.

I walk her into her apartment and she admits, "I'm a little tipsy."

We drank at dinner at her parents' house and then we finished off a full bottle of wine on the beach. I can also feel the effects of the alcohol. "I am, too." Looking at her more closely, I can see her eyes are glassy. If we had decided that I would stay the night with her, this is a game changer. I could never take advantage of her, and I also can't leave her in this condition. "Do you have some Tylenol?"

"It's in the medicine cabinet."

"May I?"

"Go ahead. I'm sorry. I didn't mean to drink so much tonight. I swear it went right to my head."

"It's okay. I hope you had a great time."

"I always do with you."

I hope her words are genuine. I think they are. I quickly get two Tylenol and a glass of water and hand them to Grace. "Take these." She looks at me and then the pills. "Now," I say. "You'll thank me in the morning."

"I'm not that drunk," she says before taking the pills and drinking the entire glass of water.

"I know. But I think you may have a headache in the morning." I put the glass in the sink. "Lock up and I'll see you in the morning." I kiss her forehead before leaving.

Before I step off the last step, she calls my name. "James?" I turn and see her still standing at the opened door watching me. "Thank you. I had a wonderful time."

"Me, too, Grace. Go ahead and lock up before I leave."

"Good night."

I don't leave until I hear the click of the deadbolt. Realizing I've also had too much to drink, I walk the short distance to Parker and Sarah's.

When I arrived at Parker and Sarah's house last night, the two were already in bed and when I got up today, they were still in bed. To be in love and in your twenties must be grand. I think that if I had spent the night with Grace last night, no one would have known. The next morning, I get up early and shower before setting off on foot down Shell Lane. I want to make sure Grace is up, but I also need to ask Beau and Carly about using his pedal boat. I left a note for Sarah and Parker on the counter so they wouldn't question if I came home last night or not. Walking down to Beau and Carly's gives me time to think about my relationship with Grace. I wouldn't mind moving on to the next step. Not an engagement, but something where we both agree to not date other people. Is that a form of commitment? At least for a man of my age, it is. I certainly have no desire to sleep with several different women. Is it understood that once a relationship progresses that both parties are exclusive? Do I need to clarify this with her? I can't ask my son or anyone else about this. Is this something I can Google and trust to get a correct answer? Would Google even know the answer?

Beau and Carly are up with the kids when I get there and are very kind in lending me their boat.

"Do you want to stay for breakfast?" Carly asks.

I haven't eaten yet, but I'm hoping to catch Grace early enough and take her to breakfast. "Thank you, but I still have some things I need to do."

"Okay. Maybe we'll see you later."

I leave and walk in the direction of Grace's home. I get a whiff of bacon and wonder which restaurant it's coming from. Then I see Grace's balcony door open and wonder if it's coming from there. As I get closer, I hear country music coming from her apartment. On her balcony are two chairs and a small table in between them. There's a cup of steaming hot coffee and a book sitting on the table. I watch as Grace steps out onto the balcony, carrying a plate of food. She looks beautiful and happy. I stop and just watch her as she looks out into the open water. She inhales deeply the fresh salty sea air before sitting down with her breakfast. I continue walking and watching. She looks down at me and smiles.

"Good morning, James."

"Good morning, Grace." I nod. "How are you feeling today?"

"I have a slight headache, but overall I feel wonderful. Are you hungry?"

"Did you make extra?"

"I thought I might be seeing you early this morning." She picks up the hot cup of coffee and blows the steam. "Come on up, the door's unlocked. The food's in the oven and there's hot coffee in the pot or juice in the fridge if you prefer it."

I smile. "I'll be right there."

When I get my coffee and plate of food, I walk outside on the balcony to join Grace. She hasn't started eating yet. "What are you doing out and about so early on a Saturday?"

Do I tell her I wanted to make sure she was awake? I decide to keep that to myself. "I went to see Beau and Carly about using their pedal boat this afternoon."

She looks surprised. "We didn't call them last night, did we?" I shake my head as I can see last night flash in her eyes. "I think something was wrong with those marshmallows."

I scoop up some of the breakfast casserole onto my fork. "The marshmallows?"

"Yeah. It couldn't have been the alcohol. So, I'm blaming it on those white, melted, puffed balls of heaven."

I laugh at her analogy. "Did you wake up with a hangover?"

"A small one. I think the Tylenol you gave me last night probably helped. Thank you. But even though I may have consumed too much to drink, I had a great time. I've never built a fire on the beach before."

"It was a first for me, too. I also had a good time. I'm also looking forward to spending the afternoon with you on the boat."

She smiles brightly. "Me, too. Is there anything you want me to do?"

"No, I don't think so. I'll take care of the food and drinks. Just be sure to bring some sunscreen and Chapstick for yourself."

"My bag's all ready. I always have a good time with you, and I'm sure today will also be amazing."

"I hope so."

She turns serious. "You know, last weekend was incredible." I can hear a "but" or a hesitation in there somewhere. I don't say anything. "I'm not sure how to handle *us* while on the island. We never talked about telling our kids." She pauses and laughs. "I just heard how that sounds. Do we have to tell our kids anything?"

"Grace, I just honestly had this same conversation with myself on the way over here."

"You did?"

"I did." I set my coffee down and look at her. "Last weekend was amazing for me and I'd like to see you exclusively. Is that something you'd consider?"

"Good. Yes. I'd like that."

"Good." My dilemma's done. "Then how about when we're on the island we just hang out and whatever happens, happens?"

"Okay, I can live with that."

"Good. And for the record, Parker and Sarah were still in bed last night when I got there and they were still in bed when I left this morning." I take a bite of my food as that sinks in.

"You mean they wouldn't have known if you didn't come home last night?" I just look at her. "You mean you could have stayed the night with me and no one would have known?"

I just smile. "That's what it means."

"Well, that sucks."

"I couldn't agree more. I was thinking about maybe on Friday you can come to Charlotte for the weekend."

A smile forms on her face. "Next week can't come fast enough."

After breakfast, I offer to help clean up, but she refuses my assistance. There wasn't a huge mess to clean up.

I kiss her goodbye. "I'll see you at noon."

"I'm excited. I'll be ready."

I leave and walk over to the market that Tony owns to order our lunch. Tony greets me warmly. "There's the good doctor." It used to embarrass me when people called me "doctor" outside of the office, but now I feel like they use the word just as they would words like "sir," "man," or "Mr."

"Good morning, Tony."

"It's good seeing you today."

"Thank you, and you, too." I walk up to the deli counter.

"What can I get for you today?"

"I'll be boating later and I wanted to see about ordering a picnic lunch for later. Do you offer something like a meal combo or do I need to order a sandwich and buy everything separate?"

He waves his hand to the white overhead board behind him. "These are what I have. It'll take me a few minutes to get everything ready."

"I won't need it until noon."

"That's plenty of time." A customer walks up to the register with a cart of food.

"Look it over and let me know what you want. I'll be sure to have it ready for you by noon."

"Okay, I will. Thank you."

"If you don't see something you like, let me know. I'll find something else for you."

"That's very kind of you." For some reason I get a feeling Tony would offer this service to anyone who enters his market.

The lunches he offers are quite impressive. Some include wine or champagne, but I decide on something simple. A couple of freshly made deli subs, cups of fresh seasonal fruit, chips, cookies, and juice. I also decide to add a few extra bottles of water.

"I'll have it ready for you," Tony assures me.

"I have some time to spare. Could you tell me is there someplace around here off the beaten path I could go and hang out for a bit?"

"I have the perfect spot. Come with me." Tony walks around the counter and out the back door. He has a private deck overlooking the ocean. On the deck are a few fishing poles, a hammock, and some patio furniture. "Go fishing or hang out here for as long as you want."

"Tony, this is your personal space. I can't just barge in on you."

"Why not? I'm not using it. Go for a walk on the beach or do nothing at all. I have customers I need to tend to. Relax and enjoy. This part of the beach is private so no one should bother you."

"Are you sure?"

"Yes. Absolutely."

"Thank you."

"No thanks needed," he says, walking back into the market.

GRACE

I wasn't entirely surprised to see James this morning. I was hoping he'd be wandering about this morning before the shop opened.

The shop's been steady all morning and it's refreshing to hear compliments from the patrons on the products I make and sell.

Mom and Dad arrived earlier so I'd have enough time to get ready for an afternoon on the water with James. I had my beach bag packed and all I needed to do was change into beach wear. I decided on a navy one-piece, a blue and white sarong, with a blue and white straw hat and flip-flops.

"Did you pack sunscreen?" Dad asks.

"I did and some lip balm. Towels, a first-aid kit, a nail file, sunglasses, and a magazine. I think I have everything."

"Let's just hope you won't need the first-aid kit," Mom says, laughing.

James walks into the shop just before noon wearing board shorts and a yellow tee shirt. He's also carrying a wooden picnic basket. He looks more like a local islander or vacationer than a professional doctor. I have to admit I like this look on him, too. Once I think about it, there isn't a look that I don't like on him. Even dressed for a day on the water, I can smell his unique cologne.

"From now on I promise to plan something around Grace's schedule," James says as an apology to my parents for being here to look after the shop for me so we can go boating.

"Don't be silly. We don't mind watching the store so you two can enjoy this lovely weather. Just have a great time and the dolphins should be feeding soon. Maybe you'll get a chance to see them up close and personal," Dad says.

"That would be nice," I agree.

"Maybe we'll get lucky," James says. I quickly look away and try to get the double meaning out of my head. Up until last weekend, I hadn't had sex in twenty-two years. Maybe that's why the intimacy I shared with James was so incredible and now my appetite for intimacy is expanding. I can feel James looking at me and I wonder if he can read my mind. God, I hope not. "Do you have everything you need, Grace?" James asks.

I pick up my beach bag from the chair behind the counter. "I do and I'm ready." We bid everyone farewell and walk in the direction of Beau and Carly's. James checks his cell phone and he has a look of concern on his face. "Is everything okay?"

"I think so. I got this strange call from a girl that used to work for me and then the phone went dead."

"Did you call her back?"

"Several times and it just goes to voice mail."

"Maybe she's in a dead spot."

"Maybe. I tried leaving her a voice mail, but it says her mailbox isn't set up."

"Should you try to call her again?"

"Do you mind? I know this is *our* time."

"No. Absolutely not. You should call her."

I watch as he pushes redial, listens, and then hangs up. "Nothing."

"Try again later until you reach her."

"Are you sure you won't mind?"

I can see his concern on his face. "I'm sure. Is this something you feel the need to return back to Charlotte for?"

"No. She just sounded distraught and her words were broken up. I couldn't hear what she was saying."

"James." I stop walking and face him. "If you want to cancel this date, I'll understand."

He takes my hand and walks toward Beau and Carly's. "We have plans and I intend to keep them." He tucks his phone into his back pocket and changes the subject.

Before we get in the boat, James and I leave our cell phones at Beau and Carly's house to avoid them getting ruined by the salt water. It is also nice to not have the distraction. If our kids need us, they all know where to find us. The rest of the day is filled with boating, swimming, laughter, great food, and polite conversation.

I can tell there's something's still bothering him. "Do you want to talk about it?"

"What?"

"I can tell something's bothering you. Is it the phone call that has you upset?"

"I'm sorry. I'm not upset as much as I am concerned," he says.

"James, it's all right. If you want to talk about it, I'm a great listener."

"It's a long story."

I prop my feet up on the boat and cup my hands behind my head. "I have all day."

He laughs. "You asked for it." He tells me about a girl in his office who filed a harassment complaint against one of the male nurses who worked in his office. He goes into detail about how he didn't know who to believe. "I liked them both. They worked for me, and yet I had no idea which one was lying."

"What did you do? Fire the person whom the complaint was filed against?"

"No. He quit. He told me Anna was manipulative and then walked out the door."

"Manipulative? Did he elaborate on how?"

"No. He just left and I've never heard from him since."

"That's strange. Does he have a wife and kid?"

He looks at me. "Yes. He has a wife and very small child."

"I bet he was avoiding making headline news."

"I think so, too," he agrees. "Parker disagrees. He thinks because Matt didn't fight for his innocence that he must have had something to hide."

"Men will go to great lengths to protect their loved ones."

"I agree."

Maybe she's in trouble. "May I suggest we head back and you should try calling her again?" I also think he may want to tread lightly with her. Maybe she filed that complaint because she felt wronged, but if she's on drugs, then perhaps she filed the complaint with another kind of agenda.

"Are you done for the day?" he asks.

"My skin feels tight from the sun. I'm ready for a cool shower."

"Okay, we can head to land."

After a long day on the water, I'm not ready for this day to end. James attempts to call Anna without success. After we gather our things, we walk down Shell Lane towards my apartment. "Later, do you want to come over and watch a movie with me?"

"I would like that." He takes my hand in his. "Would you be interested in having dinner with me, first?"

I smile at his offer. "How about we have dinner and a movie at my apartment tonight? I just need time to shower and decide on something for us to eat."

"I can pick something up on my way to your house for dinner."

"Great. Is seven o'clock too late?"

"Sounds perfect. But you can come over whenever you're ready."

***

I shower and straighten up the apartment before James arrives. After applying scented lotion to my sun-dried body,

I dress in a floral sundress and forgo the shoes since we'll be staying in. If I were home alone on a Saturday night, I would light some candles, open a bottle of wine, and curl up on the couch in some loungewear and watch Lifetime movies until I fall asleep. But since James will be here, I decide to skip the loungewear. I do light some candles, open a bottle of wine, and wait patiently for him to arrive.

James arrives in white shorts and a pale blue linen shirt. He's carrying food from a nearby restaurant. He's also freshly showered and his hair is still damp. To be a man and not have to worry about your hair and makeup would be nice. He kicks his flip flops off at the door before coming in.

"These are for you." He hands me a small bouquet of flowers. "You look beautiful, by the way."

I feel a blush from his compliment. "Thank you. You don't need to bring me flowers," I say, taking the flowers from him.

"Why, you don't like roses?"

"No, I love them. But…"

"That's exactly why I should do it."

I smile as I inhale the large bouquet of yellow roses. "Thank you."

"Sorry I'm late, but the restaurant was busier than I expected."

"I should have warned you about that." I close the door after him.

"Even though I called in the order, I still had to wait."

"I should have warned you that the island restaurants are always busy on the weekends."

"It's okay. I just sat on the deck and enjoyed the view."

I watch as he removes the food from the sack. "I wasn't sure what you wanted so I got a little bit of everything."

"It smells delicious."

The dining room table already has a vintage white and lace tablecloth on it. I make sure to place the flowers James bought me in the center before lighting the candles.

As we sit and eat, I don't ask James about the phone call from earlier. I don't want to sour the mood.

"Can I get you some more wine?" James asks.

I begin to stand. "I can get it."

"Please, allow me." After he refills both of the wine glasses he says, "I enjoyed myself with you on the boat today."

I look from one of his eyes to the other. "I did, too."

After dinner, we have dessert and coffee outside on the balcony. The sun has already set and the hustle and bustle of the shops is dying down. When the night air becomes too cool and the wind picks up, we go inside. James closes the French doors leading from the balcony. We sit on the couch and watch *You've Got Mail* with Meg Ryan and Tom Hanks. This is my one of my favorite movies so when James was movie searching on the television and stopped on this movie, I was excited. It turns out that he's also a huge Meg Ryan and Tom Hanks fan.

During the movie, James and I sit close. He holds my hand often and once he also puts his arm around me. It's nice having him close to me. Touching me softly as he intertwines our fingers. When I get sleepy, I feel comfortable enough to rest my head on his shoulder. When I feel him looking down at me to see if I'm asleep, I look up at him. Our eyes meet and he leans down and kisses me. It's soft and sensual. No words are spoken; we just share a soft intimate kiss.

He pulls away and stares at me before saying, "You're the most beautiful woman in the world."

I stare back at him and try to remember the last time anyone has ever said those words to me. It doesn't take long for the kiss to deepen and become more intense. In one fluid motion he lifts me up and places me on his lap. While straddling his legs, I wrap my arms around his neck and pull him closer to me. James makes me feel beautiful and alive. He makes me remember what it's like to be a woman, and tonight I need that. I like his strong arms wrapped securely around me. I like the feel of his lips on mine. His tongue enters my mouth softly and soon I want more. I want him and everything he has to offer me on this night. I want to feel loved even if only for a few hours.

Between heavy breaths, I say, "Stay with me."

JAMES

The night with Grace was magical. I wanted to take things slowly with her, but when she looked up at me I knew I had to have her. Again. She isn't like other women I've dated. She doesn't care about wealth or prestige. She cares about her children and their happiness. She cares about her health and happiness and the little things that life has to offer. A movie night at home, not a weekend cruise to the Bahamas. Hunting sea glass, not shopping for jewelry at Kays. She's definitely a rare find.

Although I spent the night, neither of us got much sleep. Love making was something we both wanted and needed. I know last night was unexpected, but it didn't take anything from it. It was amazing and I hate to see it end. Grace is insatiable and I'll never have enough time with her.

In the morning instead of rushing out the door so she could get ready for church like I thought she would, we have a leisurely breakfast at her place. I like seeing her in her element. At home in white yoga pants and a pink tank top. We prepare breakfast together: pancakes, bacon, eggs, and fresh fruit.

We don't discuss what I'll tell Parker when he asks where I was. We don't discuss what she'll tell Sarah when she asks and we know they will. They'll know I didn't come home last night when I walk into their house this morning. Will they assume I was with Grace? I hope so since she's the only person I'm seeing. But do they know how serious it's gotten in the short time I've been with her? My only concern is Grace's reputation. Maybe I should have left her house sooner, but I couldn't leave. Well, I could have, but I didn't want to. I'm a selfish bastard and I wanted all the time with her I could get.

Just before nine, I decide I need to leave. Grace and I still need to get ready for church. I'm glad I'll be making the walk of shame and not Grace. It must be terrible for the woman to get dressed and leave in the morning after such an intimate night together. But for me it's not a walk of shame: I'll be walking home proudly with my head held high. I feel like Grace and I are now in a relationship and I couldn't be happier. I'd rent a billboard and post my new relationship status on it if doing this were socially acceptable. But I think that could be social suicide.

I stand in the doorway and kiss her goodbye. I don't thank her or tell her I had a great time. It doesn't seem appropriate to say those words. "I'll see you soon." I thought about asking her if we could just skip church today but decided against it. I've been stalling as I know when I leave the church, I'll be heading back home to Charlotte. I like my time here on the island and my time I get to spend with Grace although it's never nearly enough.

She stands on her tiptoes and kisses me again. "I'll see you at church." It doesn't go unnoticed that she doesn't thank me either. It just wouldn't seem right. Still, a simple "thank you, Tarzan or Stud" would be nice. Our night together was a mutual decision and one not made in the heat of passion that was later a regret. Just like last weekend it was incredible.

I lightly touch her cheek and chin before kissing her one last time.

Of course, when I get to Parker and Sarah's house, they're sitting at the table having breakfast. Parker glares at me when I walk past while Sarah just smiles.

I quickly shower and dress for church. Other than looks, no one mentioned my absence last night. I think Parker wanted to but we never had any time alone. I made sure Sarah was always close. Parker's displeasure is known and it shows on his face. I feel bad but not bad enough to stop seeing Grace.

CHAPTER 7

JAMES

On my way home from church, I get a call from the Charlotte Police Department.

"When can you come in for questioning?" the detective asks.

"Questioning? For what?" I have no idea what he's talking about. Maybe he has the wrong person.

"Someone filed a sexual harassment complaint against you saying you've been harassing her at work for some time."

What? Who? In all my years as a doctor and in my entire life, I've never had a complaint or charges filed against me. This is absurd. Who would do such a thing? At work? Was it one of my employees? Was it one of my patients? I've watched *Law and Order* enough that this frightens me. "May I ask who?"

"We'll go into that once you get here."

"This sounds serious." I've done nothing wrong. "Do I need an attorney?"

"Only if you're guilty."

GRACE

After church and when I say my goodbyes to James, I follow Mom and Dad to their house for a leisurely Sunday afternoon with them, Carly and Sarah, and their families. Tony also came here to spend time with us. I didn't ask James to stay since I knew he had a long drive back.

I feel differently today than I usually do. Maybe because my relationship with James is blossoming or maybe because I feel like I'm finally living again. My kids are happy with their lives and with their relationships, my grandkids are happy and healthy, and my parents are healthy and content with where they are in their lives. Life is good for everyone.

During Myra and Maria's nap time, we talk about Parker and Sarah's wedding plans. She's so indecisive. She doesn't know if she wants a big wedding or a small wedding. She doesn't know if she wants a beach wedding or a church wedding. Parker will go along with anything as long as he has a wife at the end of the ceremony. Whatever Sarah wants, Parker wants. I think he'd be happy with going to the Justice of the Peace in Charlotte tomorrow.

"You know," Mom says, "when I was pregnant with your mother, I couldn't decide if I wanted steak or eggs for breakfast."

All eyes turn to Sarah and Parker. Does Mom know something I don't know? Is Sarah keeping a secret from the family?

Carly speaks first. "Spill it, sister."

"There's nothing to spill," Sarah says, looking almost frightened. Parker takes her hand in his.

Is she pregnant and is that why she looks fearful? If she is pregnant, maybe she doesn't know it. Or if she is pregnant, maybe she isn't ready to share the news yet. I'm not sure I believe her. But I also don't think this is a good time to talk to either of them.

Mom says, "I'm not saying anyone's pregnant, but it was an observation concerning your indecisiveness."

"Gram, it's just so much to consider. We have a small family and Parker has even a smaller family. We get only one chance at a wedding and I want to make sure we do it right."

Maybe she isn't pregnant.

Dad says, "Sarah, have the wedding you and Parker want. If you want to get married at sunrise, do it. If you want a moonlit wedding at midnight, do that. This is your and Parker's wedding. No other opinions matter."

"I guess we need more time to talk about it. The only thing I know for sure is, I want Beau to perform the ceremony and I want Pap to walk me down the aisle." Beau looks shocked so I guess Sarah never discussed this with him. "That is if Beau wants to. I never actually asked him."

"Sarah, it would be my honor to wed you and Parker."

Since Michael's dead, it makes sense that her Pap would give her away.

"I wouldn't have it any other way," Dad says.

Sarah stands and walks over to hug him and Beau. "Thank you both."

***

With the temperatures rising, more and more people are flocking to Seashell Island to enjoy their weekends, holidays, and time away from the city.

I'm busy through the day and exhausted at night. James usually calls me mid-week to check in and see how things are going. So, when he doesn't call on Thursday I decide to call him.

"Just checking in to see how you are," I say.

"I've had a busy week, sorry I haven't called. How is everything?" he asks.

He sounds tired.

I try to keep my tone even. "It's good but you sound tired so I won't keep you. I guess I'll see you Friday for dinner then."

"About that, Grace. I'm sorry but something's come up and I need to cancel our plans for this weekend."

"Oh." I wasn't expecting that. "That's okay. Well, I guess I'll see you next weekend then."

"I hope to have everything sorted out by then."

Maybe he sounds defeated and not tired like I originally thought. "Is there something I can do to help?"

"I wish, but no. I'll try to call you this weekend."

"Okay, enjoy the rest of your week."

"You, too."

He hangs up. This call isn't what I was expecting. He seemed distant. On edge maybe. Maybe I'm reading too much into this. Maybe he's just busy and something's come up like he said. I'll see if Parker or Sarah mentions him this weekend.

On Friday, Mom and Dad deliver some fresh potted hanging baskets filled with beautiful greenery and red geraniums to Carly's bookstore, Tony's market, Parker's medical practice, and to my candle and floral shop. Dad steps on the black metal hanger to secure it into the ground and then Mom hangs the beautiful overflowing basket of flowers. I look down the street and I can see other businesses are also working on their curb appeal. Carly also added a few round tables and chairs to the sidewalk outside her shop with brightly colored cushions. When someone purchases a book and a coffee from her shop, now they can hang out for a bit outside and enjoy the sea breeze, the view, and a good book.

Just after three o'clock Sarah comes over and asks, "Do you need any help?"

"Aren't you working today?" She works in the office of Parker's practice. I know he's always opened on Friday so it surprises me to see her.

"I am. I mean I was. Parker closed early so he could be with his dad."

"James? What's wrong with James?"

She looks concerned. "I don't know, but it's something big."

"What do you mean?" I look around and I'm thankful when I see no customers in the shop.

"Parker called his dad this week like he does every week, but this time he left the room to talk to him."

"I don't see how that's cause for alarm."

"James was with his attorney and Parker wouldn't tell me why. Then today he tells me he needs to be with his father this weekend and Parker asked us to reschedule his appointments for Monday and Tuesday."

"Is James in trouble?" What kind of trouble would James be in? A speeding ticket? Jaywalking? You wouldn't need an attorney for that. "Maybe it's a DUI." I doubt that. After our fire on the beach and a bottle of wine, he wouldn't even drive from my house to his son's and it was only a couple blocks away.

"That's serious, but I think it's more serious than that."

She's right, but what could it be? "Sarah, will you mind the store while I run upstairs? I need to restock the candles."

"You're calling James first, right?"

"You betcha."

JAMES

It's been nearly two weeks since I got that dreadful phone call from the Charlotte Police Department about these bogus sexual harassment complaints. Anna filed a complaint with the police department and with the EEOC. That stands for Equal Employment Opportunity Commission. I've been asked to not be in contact with Anna for any reason. So, I have no answers as to why she would accuse me of such wrongdoing. Matt said she was manipulative, but that's all he said. What does that mean?

The first thing I did was call my attorney, then I called Parker. These accusations are bogus and this could destroy my reputation and my career. I needed to find a way to clear my name and I needed to do it quickly. If and when this makes the front page of Charlotte's main newspaper, everything I've worked hard for will be finished. My good name will be trashed.

Why would Anna do this to me? I've met with the detectives and they had Anna's phone records of the day Grace and I went boating. They had proof where I called her repeatedly. Proof of the voice mails where I asked her to "Call me." I told them the truth. That she called me and was distraught before the phone went dead. I was worried so I called her back, repeatedly, to check on her wellbeing. I also told them about her tardiness at work. I realize now that I should have asked the police to do a wellness check on her.

Sadly, my story didn't match her story. She said she called me to tell me to leave her alone and that's why I called her back so many times. The phone calls supposedly show a pattern of harassment. She also said she didn't feel safe working with me in the office so she often came in late so she wouldn't have to be there with me alone. She knew what time others came in and she'd wait for the patients to get there so there'd be witnesses to any sexual harassment.

If that wasn't bad enough, I'll also have to meet with the Medical Licensing Board to defend my actions. I could lose my medical license.

What was Anna hoping to gain from all of this? Does she know my livelihood is at stake? Does she care? What is she hoping to gain? If she's on drugs, wouldn't this be about money? Why hasn't she reached out to me?

The next morning, I decide I need to call Grace. She deserves the truth.

"Hey, James," she answers. "I just saw the newspaper. What's going on?"

What does she mean she just saw the newspaper? "What's in the paper, Grace?"

"You didn't see it?"

"Hold on a second while I get the paper from the front porch." My picture is on the front page along with this headline: "Local doctor charged with sexual harassment."

"I'm innocent, I swear."

"Does this have to do with the girl in your office?"

I don't answer. "I have a feeling that things are going to get messy and I think it's best that we stop seeing each other until I can clear my name." If I can ever clear my name.

"James, you didn't answer me."

"Grace, it's best to not involve you. I need to go." I just disconnect the call.

***

When I see Grace's name on my cell phone a few days later, I decline the call. She deserves better than me. Guilty or not, it doesn't look or sound good, and if I were her, I would run far and fast from a man accused of sexual harassment or misconduct. Especially a doctor harassing one of his employees.

I show up for work earlier than usual. The work phone rings so I answer it thinking it could be from a patient.

"Doctor Taylor speaking."

"Doctor James Taylor, this is Anna." My heart skips a beat. She says, "A heavy bag of money will make all this go away."

"What are you talking about?"

"Money, Benjamins, greenbacks, moolah, cash. You get the picture, Doc?"

"You want me to pay you to make these false accusations to go away?"

"Yes, that's right. Matt paid up quickly and you should, too."

Matt paid her? This is news to me. I don't trust that if I pay her she'll just go away. I imagine she'll be back for more money with even more serious accusations.

"Anna?" I say slowly, "I'm not paying you one thin dime or even one red cent."

I hang up the phone and hope that I did the right thing. I also call the police to report the phone call.

At the beginning of the work day, I decide to tell Julie, my office manager. She's been with me since the start of my business. She deserves to hear it from me. To also know about the accusations Anna made against Matt.

"Anna's the culprit," Julie says, standing near the door in the patients' waiting area.

"She is."

"This is bullshit."

"I agree."

Julie says, "And it comes at a perfect timing."

Perfect timing? "You lost me."

"You know with the Hollywood scandal with women coming forward saying they were sexually abused or assaulted ten, twenty, and some of them are even accusing men of molesting them thirty years ago." She takes a step forward. "Now everyone's sympathetic to all women: innocent or not. We hear that we should believe all women when they claim to have experienced sexual harassment. I believe that husbands, boyfriends, and close relatives should believe them, but I also believe that police officers and government officials should take each claim seriously and investigate it to see if it is true, as in many cases it is — but in some cases it's not. Law is one of Humankind's most important inventions, and I believe in the rule of law. No one's life should be ruined by a claim of sexual harassment unsupported by real evidence."

"You have a point. I guess it is perfect timing on her part."

"What does she want? Money?"

I take a step closer to Julie. "How did you know?"

"YOU TALKED TO HER!"

"She called the office this morning. When she demanded money, I quickly hung up."

She asks, "Did you at least record the phone call she made to your cell phone?"

"No. How could I do that? We weren't face to face where I could record our conversation."

"There are some phone apps that when downloaded, they instantly record every phone call, incoming and outgoing from your phone number."

This concerns me since I know it's illegal in some states to record people's conversations unless they know about it first. How can she know about this app? "Julie, how do you know that?"

"When my son Desmond went to basic training, another Army mom told me about the app so I could record his phone calls. You know, so I could listen to his voice when I missed him." She shifts in her seat. "Did you at least report the call to the police?"

"I did. Let's hope it'll help my case."

She stands and walks toward the reception desk. "If she's desperate for money, she'll contact you again. Download the app so you have it if you ever need it."

"I will. Thank you."

The morning my photo was in the newspaper, the office had several cancellations. I was afraid this would happen. I would have hoped the regulars would know me well enough to still have faith in me. A few men but mostly my women patients cancelled. I hope this isn't a preview of what to expect, but I have a feeling this is going to be a downhill spiral from here on out.

The next morning when I come to work, Julie is already here. This isn't unusual but she's acting different today. I noticed some things on my desk have been moved around and fewer patients' charts have been pulled and placed on my desk.

Today, I get a certified letter from the Medical Licensing Board wanting me to meet with them about the complaint. I suspected this was coming, but seeing it in writing makes it all too real. To think that I could lose my medical license over a lie is disheartening. Never did I imagine this nightmare could be my life. I feel sorry for the innocent people accused of such heinous crimes. Men and women.

When more patients cancel their appointments for today and later into the month, I realize it's time for me to close my practice. With a decline in patients, I won't be able to afford to keep the staff. One of my nurses already put her notice in yesterday that was effective immediately. She's young and she doesn't know me all that well.

I have a meeting after work to announce to the staff that I'll be closing the office in a few weeks. This won't be an easy transition for anyone. The patients who stayed with me will be required to find another doctor. My staff will need to find other employment. And I need to realize that this is the end of my medical career. Even if the medical board doesn't suspend my license, my reputation is ruined. It's tarnished, at least here in Charlotte.

The meeting was somber and when I couldn't speak, Julie spoke for me. I'm so grateful for her commitment and dedication to not just me but to my business, my staff, and to my patients. Even when I hit rock bottom, she's still trying to keep the morale up at work for the staff. I can never thank her enough. If she for one second believed the lies that Anna was telling, she would surely walk out, taking the staff and the patients with her.

To my surprise, most of my office staff said they would stay with me till the end. Some of the newer staff members put their notice in so they could find employment quickly, while a couple of nurses left without saying a word. Whatever happened to innocent until proven guilty?

"When do you meet with the board?" Julie asks as we walk out to the car together.

"In two weeks."

"It's not much time," she says sadly.

"No, it's not."

"I think we need to find Matt. Maybe he'll tell us what he knows about Anna."

"I've already been looking for him." I push the key fob to unlock my car door.

"Maybe he's on one of those popular social media sites."

"That's a very good idea, but if he is he isn't using his real name."

"I guess he wouldn't. He doesn't want Anna to find him." She stops walking and says, "Do you know his wife's maiden name? If's he's still on social media, and almost everyone is, he may be using her last name," she says.

I try briefly to recall her last name and I can't. "Or he's using her Facebook page. They're married so they share the same last name."

"When he started here he was single and he used his then girlfriend as his emergency contact," she says. "I'm going to go back inside and look up his online application."

"That's a great idea. I'll come with you."

"No, you go on," she says. "I can do it."

"Thank you," I say. And I don't just mean for her going back into the office to look for Matt's job application but I'm thanking her for standing by me.

She hugs me out in the parking lot. I'm concerned whether someone will interpret this as sexual harassment but she doesn't seem to care. I'm taken aback by her gesture. Before the allegations I would have returned her hug, but now I'm nearly afraid to touch her.

"I'm not letting go until you hug me back." I laugh because I know she means it. I wrap my arms around her and squeeze before I loosen my grip around her. "I'm not giving up and neither should you."

"I'm trying," I say, getting into my car and driving off.

I think through everything that's been going on, and my biggest loss is Grace. She's tried to call me a few times but I've neglected her calls. She deserves better. I have nothing to offer her now. And I'm sure she also questions my misconduct. Maybe if she had more time to get to know me, she would have believed me from the beginning.

I'm so thankful for the support of Parker, Sarah, Julie, some of my long-term patients, and a few staff members. I also have some colleagues and friends who are standing beside me. They probably know and fear that this could also happen to them.

Over the past several days I've received several phone calls from a private number that I've refused to answer. I suspect they're from Anna, but of course, the private phone calls could also have been from people who read the newspaper article and are calling to voice their animosity about my "reported harassment." I still consult my attorney on everything that's been going on. He suggests that I change my personal cell phone number, so I do. Of course, if the calls are from Anna, she can still call the office phone and the staff could be a witness to her calling if I put her on speakerphone.

No matter what happens, I decide to close the office on the Friday before the meeting with the medical board on the following Monday. It'll give me the weekend to pack up the office and to forward the remaining patients' charts to their new physician.

Over the next few weeks, Julie and I begin cleaning out the office. We take a few things to a storage unit every night when we leave. I've always imagined a long medical career and one that I would be forced to leave. Not forced to leave because of lies, but because I was too old to work. I love my job and what I do. I love people and helping them. And I love my committed staff; they're like my family.

"I'm going to miss walking in here on Monday," Julie says and the others agree.

"Me, too," I agree. "Do you have plans for your future?"

Julie smiles a sad smile. "I may retire on this small quaint little island called Seashell Island."

I laugh at the thought. "You would like it there."

"I know. I see the pictures Parker posts, and it looks like something right out of a vacation book."

"It is."

"What are your plans?"

"I'm not sure what I'll do. I thought about vacationing in Florida for a bit. If I like it, maybe I'll buy a bungalow and call it home."

"What about your lady friend? The one you were singing karaoke with?"

"I broke up with her."

"Over this?"

"It wasn't fair to drag her into this mess. She's a sweet lady, and she's probably never been exposed to such things."

"Really, James? She lives in today's world. She knows about lies, deception, and corruption, even if she does live a sheltered life. She isn't stupid."

"No, she sure isn't."

Julie stands and says, "I need to go to my hot yoga class, but do you need any help carrying the last of the boxes to your car?"

"No, I can get it. Parker should be here soon."

"Okay. I'll see you on Monday."

"At the medical board?"

She looks confused. "Yes, where else?" When I don't answer, she says, "I hear they're like rabid dogs. You didn't think I'd let you face them alone, did you?"

I never really thought about it. "Julie, you know it's not like a court room, open to the public. It'll be a closed meeting. They won't let you in."

"I know. But you'll see my support when you enter the room and you'll see my continued support when you exit."

What did I do to deserve her? I fight the lump in my throat. Parker also said he would be there although I never asked.

"Thank you for everything, Julie. You'll never know how much your loyalty means to me."

"I think I do and you never need to thank me for believing in you." She leans toward me for a hug and kisses me on the cheek. "I'll be back here Sunday at seven o'clock to do one last walkthrough before we hand the keys over to the leasing agent."

"Okay, thank you." I watch as she pulls out of the parking lot before I return to my office to pack up the last of my medical books. I hear the bell chime over the door and say, "Parker, I'm back here." When I hear the footsteps get closer, I'm surprised to see it's not Parker standing in my doorway, it's Anna.

CHAPTER 8

GRACE

When James told me what was going on, I couldn't believe it. I couldn't believe he was capable of such a thing. But how well do I know him? Do I know without doubt that he's innocent?

I hung up the phone and prayed for guidance. I couldn't be with a man I didn't trust. But I still felt that something wasn't right. He didn't go into detail; he just said that someone was accusing him of sexual harassment or sexual misconduct. It's the same thing, isn't it?

Over the last few weeks, I've prayed long and hard. I meditated and went deep into my soul searching for answers. If he was capable of that, wouldn't I have known it from his actions? He was never flirtatious with other women when we were out. He always gave me his undivided attention as if I were the only woman on the planet.

I've been indecisive. I don't know what to believe. Who to believe? I read the newspaper article once before tearing it into tiny little pieces and throwing it away. I couldn't look at it for another second. I felt that the James I knew could never have been capable of making any woman feel uncomfortable with his words or his actions.

On Saturday I think about the kind of man that James is, and about the kind of man that Parker is. There were no warning signs, no red flags, no alarms or bells alerting me of danger. James and Parker help out and donate money and their time to the children's home where Parker lived after his mother's death. It takes someone with a big heart to care for so many children without mothers, fathers, and families. Orphaned kids who have nowhere else to go because of their adolescent ages.

I need to know more about these accusations. I need to know more about the woman who filed the complaint against James.

I've tried to call James and he either doesn't answer my call or we talk briefly before he needs to go. I think it's his way of breaking up with me without actually saying it. Sarah said they've talked but James mostly talks to Parker.

I call Sarah and she tells me Parker's in Charlotte with his dad.

"Why didn't you go with him?" I ask.

"James didn't want anyone there with him."

"Where? At his house?"

"Yes, he's embarrassed and doesn't want me there. He's innocent, Mom."

"Can he prove it?" I ask. I need to know. I don't know why I didn't believe him sooner.

"I don't know. James has told me very little and Parker doesn't talk about it." Sarah sounds sorrowful over the phone. "I've read the article the newspaper posted and I don't believe any of it."

It is hard to believe. "Was it just the one article?"

"I know of only the one article. I cancelled the subscription we had for the *Charlotte Times*. I don't want to read that garbage."

"I stopped reading the newspaper as well. Let's just pray that the truth comes out and soon."

"Mom, you stopped talking to him. Is it because you think he's guilty?"

"He called me and broke up with me." Do I tell her that I've called him a few times since then and he hasn't answered any of my calls? "I haven't spoken to him since. But to answer your question, no, Sarah. I don't." And that's the honest truth. "I need to go."

"Where are you going?" she asks.

"To Charlotte. I need to see if there's anything I can do to prove his innocence."

"Wait for me. I'm coming with you."

I hang up and quickly pack an overnight bag with outfits for a few days. I don't know why I didn't believe in James sooner. I just hope it's not too late for us to find something that'll prove his innocence. If he's guilty of sexual harassment, then every man who has ever shaken a woman's hand must also be a harasser. I know deep in my heart that James is innocent.

I put a closed sign in the shop's window and call Mom to tell her I won't be in town for a few days. She offered for her and Dad to run the shop but it's not necessary. This is my business and my obligation, not theirs. They have a spare key and I'm pretty sure they'll be there in my absence although I did tell them not to.

I pick up Sarah, and we talk the entire way to Charlotte. She tells me about James' meeting with the medical board on Monday. No matter how this visit goes, I plan on attending the meeting or at least I'll be there to show my support. I doubt they let just anyone inside. Sarah wanted to call Parker to let him know we are on our way, but I thought it was best to keep it to ourselves. James may not want me there.

"What are we going to do if we can't prove his innocence?" Sarah asks. "He stands to lose his livelihood but more important, his reputation."

"We will. We have to. A woman in love will do anything to prove the man she loves is innocent."

My head spins in confusion at the realization that I just confessed to my daughter that I'm in love with her fiancé's father. Am I really in love with him? Is it too soon? No, it's not. I knew I loved Michael right away and James is much like Michael. He's a good and decent man. I know it in my heart *and* in my soul.

"Mom? You're in love with James?"

"Yeah, Sarah. I think I am." I look over at my daughter again so I can study her reaction. This must be a shocker for her. How will she handle the news? Up until a few months ago, I'd never dated or been with anyone but her father. Now I just confessed something to her that I never even told James.

"I knew it," she says.

"You did? How? I wasn't even sure until just a minute ago."

"Your eyes," she laughs.

"Are you saying I look love struck?"

"No. Not love struck. But before all of this you definitely looked happy. Like I remember you looking in pictures with Dad."

"I did love that man. I didn't think it was possible for me to love again."

"That's why he sent you James. Because he knew James was a good fit for you."

"You think your father sent James to me."

"Well, him and God."

***

I get butterflies when we pull up at James' house. How will he feel about me being here? Will he send me away? I made hotel reservations just in case he did. I don't expect to stay the night here, but I hope he doesn't reject me without at least talking to me first. Of course, I wouldn't blame him if he did. But I would hope I needed time to process everything. Beau and Dad's sermon last Sunday helped put things in perspective. They preached about having faith and love and if you had that, trust would soon follow.

"Come on. What are you waiting for?" Sarah asks with her car door open.

With the car still running, I ask, "What if I'm not welcome?"

"What are you talking about?"

"Sarah, I had to do a lot of praying and soul searching before I realized James couldn't possibly have done what they said he did."

"I know." She looks from me up to his home. "But you know he's innocent now."

"I do, but I also think it may be too late."

"Come on. I don't think you have anything to worry about."

My heart races as Sarah rings the doorbell. If James turns me away, I deserve it. But I'm still prepared to go to his meeting on Monday with the medical board. I just hope he doesn't turn me away tonight.

The door opens and there stands James. His eyes land on me first. Sarah walks up and hugs him before walking into the house searching for Parker. I stand there waiting for him to ask me in or ask to leave.

"Grace," James says. He has dark circles under his eye and he looks exhausted.

"Hi." I don't take a step forward. In fact, I keep my distance. Part of me is too afraid to move or speak.

"What are you doing here?" He closes the door behind him as we both stand on his front porch.

"I'm sorry. I know you didn't do or say anything inappropriate to that woman." He stares at me as if trying to read my mind. When he doesn't say anything, I back away from him. "I just wanted you to know I'm sorry it took me so long to tell you that." I turn to leave when I realize it's too late to get back what we had. What we had is now over. The damage is already done.

"Where are you going?" he asks.

I turn around and face him. "I'm going to the hotel so you, Sarah, and Parker can talk."

He takes a step forward. "You don't want to come in?" He takes another step forward. "I've missed you. I know you deserve better, but it doesn't stop me from wanting you."

I close the distance. "I'm sorry it took me so long…" I begin to say.

"You have nothing to be sorry about. I'm glad you're here."

"Me, too."

He slowly and cautiously leans down and kisses me as if he's expecting to be rejected or if he's waiting for confirmation that this kiss is welcomed. It is. It's soft and sweet. Nothing like the last time we were together where the kiss was heated and filled with lust and passion, need and want.

He takes my hand and leads me into his bare house. It's nothing like the last time I was here. There are boxes lined against the wall and nothing is hanging on his walls.

"Are you moving?" I ask. Where would he be moving to? Sarah didn't mention anything to me.

"My reputation's ruined here. Even if the medical board doesn't take my medical license, I'll never be able to work in this town again. He looks sad and says, "You should sit down. We probably need to talk."

When Sarah, Parker, James, and I sit, James takes a seat across from us and keeps his distance. He tells us the whole story. Some of this I know and some of it I didn't. I can tell Sarah is hearing this for the first time. The victim is a former employee of James'. She was a devoted worker: one he could trust. Then something happened. She changed and started calling off work for various reasons. He even went as far as referring her to a specialist for her health problems. Things seemed to have gotten better with her, and she started coming in early and staying after hours helping with the filing, restocking, and even cleaning up. Then she had a relapse. After trying to work with her through her call-offs and irrational behaviors, he finally talked to her and let her go. Shortly after, she filed a complaint with the EEOC — Equal Employment Opportunity Commission — claiming discrimination and harassment.

"Did she ever ask you for money or personal favors?" I ask. There seems like there should be more to the story.

"She did. She started asking me for small amounts of money. Twenty dollars in the beginning while she was still employed. She said she needed it for gas or groceries. I hated seeing her struggle and thought if she was struggling others in the office must also be struggling. Although I knew the wages I was paying were comparable to those in the area, I decided to give everyone a raise. I didn't like thinking someone didn't have milk or bread in their home or gas in their car to get to and from work."

"Then what?" Parker asks. "She started asking for more?"

"She was content with that for a while. Then she started asking for more money claiming it was for prescription medications and medical bills."

I take it all in and then ask, "Do you know of anyone who has a vengeance against you? Someone she might know? Could this be a conspiracy between two or more co-workers or ex-coworkers or even a former patient?"

"No. I can't think of anyone specific. I mean during the length of my career I've fired people and turned away or denied drug-seeking patients who were addicted to pain medications." James looks up at me. "You believe me, don't you?"

"I do." I only wish I had believed him sooner.

Sarah leans up in her chair. "Mom, you think this could be a conspiracy?"

"I don't know. I'm just putting this out there as a possibility."

"Dad, she might be onto something. Have you considered this?"

"I have, but there's nothing to tie Anna with anyone."

My mind races with ways I can help James. "Is Anna your office manager?"

"No. Julie's my office manager and Anna was one of several nurses working for me."

"How long has Julie been with you?"

"She's not involved. She's been with me from the beginning. She's also supported me in all of this."

His office manager supported him yet I didn't. I feel terrible for this. But after he broke up with me, he never answered or returned any of my calls to him. Sarah said he was embarrassed.

If Julie's been with him from the beginning, then she's probably like family. Family would do anything for family. Maybe she knows something that James has overlooked. Maybe we all need to talk with Julie.

James runs his hands down the leg of his blue jeans.

I can tell this is making him uncomfortable. But I have one more question I need to ask. "When's the last time you talked to Anna?"

"On Friday?"

"Dad, when did you see her?" Parker asks. He sounds surprised. "Do you mean from your car as you were driving by?"

"No. She came into the office Friday night while I was clearing my things out and waiting for you."

"What did she want?" Parker asks.

"Money. She said she could make this all go away if I'd just pay her."

"What did you do? What did you say?" Parker asks.

"I told her to get out."

I'm all for standing your ground, but wouldn't it be easier to just pay her off and make all this disappear? I don't say that. If he were to pay her and the courts and people in the community got wind of it, he would look guilty in other people's eyes. Besides, maybe she was wearing a wire or this was a setup of some kind, although I highly doubt it and feel she truly just wants the money. Of course, if he would have paid her off, then she would be back asking for more money and possibly have more false allegations. Or maybe she would target other medical professionals like Parker.

"Did she leave on her own?" Sarah asks.

"She did." I know he's tired of talking about this as it's probably been the only thing he's been able to think about since all of this started. He stands and says, "I'm sure you ladies are hungry and I'm going stir crazy. How about we head out and get something for dinner?"

I stand and put on a fake smile. "That sounds good to me." But in my head, I'm making plans to talk to Julie before Monday to see if she can remember anything.

After dinner, Parker and Sarah go to bed in the spare room, leaving James and me up.

"I made hotel reservations at the Hampton Inn. I guess I should be going." I pick up my purse and start heading toward the door.

"Grace, you don't have to leave."

James looks sad and tired. I can see all of this is taking a toll on him.

"I think it's best."

"Will you be back in the morning?"

"I will." He walks me to the door and I place a gentle hand on his chest. "As soon as this is over, maybe we can pick up where we left off."

He moves his hand slowly to my face and gently and sweetly brushes his fingertip over my bottom lip. "*If* this is ever over with, I would like that."

My eyes scan his. "James? Can I ask you something?"

"Sure. You can ask me anything."

"Where do you plan to go when this is all over?"

"Honestly, I'm not sure."

JAMES

On Sunday, the day is filled with sadness. Parker spends a lot of time on his phone and computer. He's still holding out hope that something will happen to clear me. The movers came and moved all of my things into a climate-control storage room. Before heading to a hotel, I walk around my home. I knew I wouldn't live here forever, but I wasn't ready to leave it just yet. Not right now. I figured I would sell it when I retired. Well, I guess I am retired but not by choice. If they don't suspend my medical license, what will I do? Would I go back to work? Not in Charlotte. My reputation is already destroyed here. I'll be forced to go somewhere else and hope people won't recognize me.

"Are you okay, James?"

I look at Grace and smile.

"Yeah. I think I am. Just saying goodbye."

"I'm sorry." Her eyes reveal a deep, sincere sadness.

"Thank you. Me, too. I guess my time here is done."

I pick up the fish bowl that houses my fish, Sandy Bottom Pants, and head out the door.

GRACE

On Sunday night Sarah and I decide we would go to the office to get the last of the boxes that James and Parker didn't have room for. James looks tired and I think maybe he could use some time with his son.

James told us that Julie would be at the office at seven and she'd let us in to get whatever was left. He called to give her a heads up in case she didn't believe us since she's never met either of us before.

When we pull up at the office, Julie is already in the parking lot. She's older than what I thought. She's closer to my age while I expected her to be Sarah's age. Not sure why I would have assumed that. She's dressed in yoga pants and a dark sweatshirt. Her short hair is a beautiful amber color.

"You're the girl from the video." Julie greets me with a smile.

"Video?" I look at Sarah to see if Julie's talking to her.

"Karaoke? Country music songs?" she says, unlocking the closed office door.

I forgot about our special night out and the video someone posted of us singing. "Guilty," I say. "I'm Grace and this is my daughter, Sarah."

"It's nice to meet you both."

"It's nice to meet you, too."

"Are you Parker's girlfriend?" Julie asks.

"I am."

"Good, he's a great guy."

"Thank you. I think so, too."

"God, I'm gonna miss this place." I watch as Julie steps into the office for probably the last time. "How's James doing?"

Sarah speaks up. "Terrible. It's like he's just giving up."

Julie locks the door after us. "Because he closed the office and sold his condo?"

"Exactly."

Julie says sadly, "Sadly, he's expecting to lose his medical license."

"Do you think it's a possibility?" I ask.

"I don't know, but I have heard the medical board is like bulldogs. Vicious and ready to attack."

Sarah says, "But he doesn't even know where he's going after tomorrow."

"I know."

I look at the few boxes sitting on the counter before a man in uniform knocks at the door. "We'll start carrying these out while you take care of that."

"He's just here for the surveillance cameras."

I stop and watch as she lets him in. I quickly look over at Sarah. She's also looking at me.

"Did you say surveillance cameras?"

"Yes, it was a waste of time and money. They ended up being useless." The man clears his throat. "Oh, sorry. I mean they worked fine, but I was hoping to catch something that might prove James' innocence."

"Does James know about these?"

"Oh, God, no. Because of the HIPPA privacy laws, it's tricky about where you can have cameras. James would never allow cameras in his medical office. You have to protect patients' privacy but who protects the doctor and medical staff against malpractice?"

"And against sexual harassment allegations and misconduct," Sarah adds.

"That's right. Sadly, there's nothing recorded that can help him. I didn't have them installed until after Anna accused him of harassment."

My heart races with hope. I know it all depends on where the cameras were installed and facing and if they have audio. Maybe, just maybe they caught Anna and James' conversation from Friday night.

I say, "Did you know that Anna came to visit James Friday night? Here. In his office?"

"No. James never mentioned that to me. Maybe these cameras were worth every dime after all."

JAMES

Last night I got a call from a private number. Since the app was downloaded to record my phone calls, I went ahead and answered it. This time I'm hoping it's Anna calling.

"Dr. Taylor. It's Matt."

I have no idea how he got my number and frankly, I don't care. I'm just glad he called. "Matt, I've been looking for you."

"I read the article in the paper and I suspected Anna was behind it."

Is he calling to reprimand me for bad behavior? Please tell me he doesn't believe that trash the newspaper posted. "I'm innocent, I swear."

"I know, I believe you."

He does? "Thank you." I wish I had believed him when Anna accused him of the same thing. But I was torn on who and what to believe. "I owe you an apology, Matt. I'm sorry."

"Nah. You didn't do anything wrong. I walked out on you, remember?"

That's true, he did. "I didn't know who to believe and for that, I'm sorry."

"Thank you. I'm glad it worked out." There's a pause. "You know, Anna did the exact same thing to me."

I knew Anna said he paid her off to drop the allegations. "She asked you for money?"

"Twenty thousand at first."

"I'm sorry."

"I couldn't pay that if I wanted to. She was desperate and kept lowering the price and finally she asked me for five thousand and I decided it was worth it to end this nightmare. I never told anyone, but we moved shortly after." I never knew the amount he paid her. The amount didn't matter. "I didn't have the fight in me. The Board of Nursing would never have believed me."

I say the only thing I know to say. "I'm sorry."

"I sent an email and a photocopy of the check I gave to Anna for payoff to the medical board a couple weeks ago."

"I had no idea. Thank you."

"You should also know that they're requesting me there tomorrow."

I hope it's because they believe him and not to question his integrity. "I'm sorry you're involved in this."

"It's okay. I just hope I can help you."

Me, too. "So do I."

***

When my attorney and I walk into the building of the Medical Licensing Board, the waiting area is full. It's full of my friends, colleagues, my staff members, business owners of businesses I frequent, and former patients. People are holding signs protesting my innocence. Some are wearing shirts with my photo and "falsely accused" written across the top. I've had people reach out to me through phone calls and e-mails wishing me well and offering support. But I never expected this. I'm overwhelmed, I'm shocked at all of the familiar faces, and I'm filled with gratitude for the show of support and the love in this room.

I'm not sure whether this will or won't affect the decision the board will make. But it doesn't matter. They are here to show their support and for that, I'm thankful.

I came early so I could sit in quiet and reflect on my life. The good and the bad. But instead I walk around the room thanking everyone who came.

I asked Parker, Sarah, Grace, and Julie to come just before ten o'clock. I couldn't look at their sad faces. I also didn't want them to see me. I'm nearly broken. This has nearly destroyed my soul. I've always done what was right. I've always been by the book. And yet a lie has the power to ruin me. I'm trying to keep the faith, but it's hard. I'm losing all hope in mankind and womankind. I'm losing hope in the system and in the laws.

My tie feels like a noose, my jacket feels like a straightjacket, and my mouth feels like the Sahara Desert. As far as I can tell, my breathing is calm and steady. I'm at least thankful for that. Maybe I appear to look normal although I feel anything but. My life is in the hands of a medical board of strangers. How many of them will decide my fate? I don't know. I never thought I would be facing anyone from a disciplinary committee.

Just then I hear commotion near the front door. I turn slightly as I watch Parker, Sarah, Grace, and Julie storm through the doors. Grace, Sarah, and Julie walk to me while Parker heads over to get my attorney.

"We have proof she's lying," Sarah says.

Do I dare hope for good news?

"It's true. We do," Julie confirms. She looks at me with a genuine smile.

I ask Grace, "What's going on?"

"Julie installed cameras in the office after Anna made the complaints on you."

I look at Julie and my first thought is, she's crazy. What about HIPPA? What about the patients' privacy? You can't record people's medical problems. You can't have them on video as you give them a diagnosis. It's private, and medical professionals can go to prison for doing that. Then my second thought is, hug her for using her brilliant mind and for saving my ass.

"You got her on video from Friday night?" I ask, looking only at Julie.

"I did."

My attorney asks, "Wait? What? Anna was in your office on Friday? Why didn't you tell me?"

"It would be all hearsay. I didn't have any witnesses, and it would be my word against hers."

"What's on the tape?" the attorney asks.

"Enough to clear James of all allegations," Julie states candidly.

I look over at Julie. "You're just finding out about this now?"

"No. We found it last night but it took until this morning for the CCTV guy to get me digital recording from the surveillance camera."

I want to kiss her but I'm not going there. My face lights up with hope. I look at Parker and then to my attorney. Is it too late to give proof to the board? "Is it too late to show the medical board proof?"

My attorney says, "I hope not."

"I also have some good news," I say, looking around the room for Matt. I get worried when I don't see him.

"You found Matt?" Julie asks.

"Matt called me last night." I don't discuss what we talked about.

"Can he help you?"

"Yes, I think so." I hope so. "He'll be here today."

The large double oak doors open and they call my name. "James Parker Taylor. We're ready."

My heart beats faster. "Time will tell." I scan the room looking for Matt when I realize he isn't here.

"Good luck, Dad."

"Thank you, Parker and thank you all for being here." I look around the room before walking through the large oak doors with my attorney by my side. My attorney and I walk into the room, and I see Matt already seated at a mahogany table.

CHAPTER 9

JAMES

After what feels like hours, I walk out of the room a free man with Matt and my attorney by my side. "No disciplinary action was needed," I announce to the room full of supporters. The room erupts with excited chatter.

On the tape was audio and video. The audio was so clear that you could nearly hear the tick of the clock on the wall. Anna was demanding money to drop the charges against me just as she did to Matt. At first, she was asking for fifty thousand dollars but now she was asking for twenty thousand. She appeared desperate. She threatened that if I didn't pay her, she would make more serious allegations against me. I kept asking her to leave but she refused.

Matt says, "I need to get back to my wife and kid. I'm glad everything worked out for you."

He offers me a solid firm handshake. "Thank you for everything."

"You're welcome." He talks briefly to Julie before he leaves.

"Thank you," I say to Julie in a cracked but excited voice. She walks over and hugs me. I can see Sarah smiling and Grace has tears in her eyes. I'm hugging a woman, a friend, a former employee with no fear that this will be misinterpreted as harassment. It feels good. My life flashes before me. I thought it was nearly over. I sold my home, closed my business, and placed everything I own in storage for a life of uncertainty.

After I hug Julie, I hug Sarah next. She's never doubted me and was willing to do whatever she could to prove my innocence. I have no doubt that she'll make my son a wonderful wife and will always stand beside him no matter what problems may cross his path.

Next, I slowly walk over to Grace. Sadness or maybe guilt fills her eyes. She has no reason to feel guilty for anything. I want to hug her, but I want to go slowly. She hugs me before I have time to ponder anything else. I embrace her small frame with both of my arms and savor the moment. I didn't think this would ever happen again. Until the other night, I thought my time with Grace was over and it wasn't nearly long enough. I wanted more time with her. I needed more time with her to learn as much as I could about her.

"I'm sorry," she whispers.

"You have nothing to be sorry about."

Before we leave, I thank everyone who took time out of their busy day to show their support. Once everything is said and done, we go to a secluded restaurant to celebrate.

"James, what are your plans now?" Julie asks.

I hold Grace's hand under the table. "I'm homeless and jobless. I don't really have any plans. I think I need to come up with something and soon."

"You could always buy another condo and reopen your practice."

She's right, I could do that, but …. "I think my time here, in Charlotte, is done. The accusations proved to be false, but my reputation's tarnished. No matter how much time passes, it'll never be completely repaired." I decide to change the subject from me to her. "What about you? Have you found a new job?"

"No. I'm not looking. The more I thought about retirement, the better it sounded. And with the generous severance package you gave me, I have enough money and time that I could actually travel a bit. That's something I always wanted to do. Tour Italy and maybe visit a quaint little place called Seashell Island."

"You would like it there. I haven't met a single person who was disappointed in the area."

Julie smiles. "So let's say if I were to visit there next week, what would be my chance of running into you there?"

I hope pretty good, but what should I say? Grace and I haven't really talked about it. My son lives there, so of course I'll be there from time to time seeing him.

Grace reaches into her purse with her free hand. "Here's my business card. If you're in the area, please stop by. I'm sure I'll have a way of contacting him."

Julie takes the card. "Thank you, Grace. I'm sure I'll be seeing you around."

***

Later that night at the hotel, Grace and I talk. "I'm happy things worked out for you today."

I intertwine our fingers. "Thank you."

Grace pauses as if in deep thought. "I know this is forward of me, but I'd like for you to come back to the island with me."

I know this is a big step for Grace. I run my fingers along her beautiful full lips. "I need some time, Grace. I hope you can understand that."

"Is it because I didn't believe you were innocent? It took me about a day to realize you couldn't have done or said anything inappropriate to that woman or to any other woman. I tried calling you but you wouldn't accept my calls."

Tears stream down her pale cheeks. She's right. I didn't return her calls or listen to her voice mail messages.

"No, Grace. That's not why. I understand your hesitation. You have every right to question her accusation."

"Then what is it? I know we can work out whatever it is."

I don't know how to put it into words. "This past month has opened my eyes and I just need some time to put it all into perspective." I release her hand and crack my knuckles. "I just need some time to figure it out."

"Okay. I understand." The stream of tears running down her cheeks tells me she doesn't. "Will I see you again? Will you be back?"

I lean in and kiss her sweetly. "Yes, I promise you I'll be back as soon as I get it all figured out."

GRACE

After a long talk, James walks me back to my room. He promised me he'd be back, but I'm not sure I believe him. I didn't ask where he was going. I wanted to, but I thought if he wanted me to know then he would tell me.

The next morning, I meet Sarah and Parker in the lobby of the hotel. I look around for James and when I don't see him, I decide he must be running late or he's getting the car since I see James' Beta fish, Sandy Bottom Pants, in her fish bowl of water on the counter.

"Where's your dad?"

He looks at Sarah before looking back at me. "He left earlier this morning."

My heart falls to the pit of my stomach. My eyes sting from unshed tears. "He's gone?" I thought I would see him this morning. I didn't know last night would be my last time with him.

"I'm sorry, Grace," Parker says softly.

I sit down before I fall down. "I should have believed him." The tears stream down my face. "I should have been there to support him. He's one of the kindest men I've ever met and I doubted him."

"Grace," Parker says, taking my hand in his, "he understood. He really did. Dad just needs time to figure out what he'll do from here on out."

"He could move to the island and work with you. He could live with me. I love him." The tears continue to fall. "I never had the chance to tell him, but I do. Now I may never get the chance." I feel broken. I feel responsible for James leaving. My heart can't take another pain like this. It's like losing Michael all over again. But I feel responsible for this pain.

"C'mon, Mom. I'll drive you home while Parker takes our car."

I walk over to the counter, blurry eyed, and take James' fish, Sandy Bottom Pants, with me.

***

It's been a month since I've seen or heard anything from James. One month since he walked out of my life. One month since his good name was cleared of any wrongdoing. That's a lie. His reputation is ruined, but it's been a month since he was cleared of any harassment.

Since James left, there was a newspaper article clearing his name. It was small in comparison to the first article when the allegations first surfaced. I guess they thought it was more important to slander his name instead of clearing it.

Lots of people who read the first article won't even see the second article. I found it strange since it was posted on the same day as another doctor was found guilty in a court of law for rape. That article was front and center, where it should have been, but James' article was on the third page near the bottom.

Although it would be so easy for me to fall into a dark depression, I fight daily to stay in the light. It's been a daily fight to do the simple things in life. Cleaning, eating, and showering are chores. Then I must wear a happy face while I work. I have to admit that the customers make it easy to smile. My granddaughters and my children also make it easier. But then darkness rolls in, everyone goes home, and I close up my shop and go to my lonely apartment.

Against my better judgment, I tried to call James. I thought if we could talk and I told him how I felt maybe he'd come back to me. Maybe I could help him work out whatever was troubling him. But instead of my talking to him, a man answered stating this was his new cell phone number. Speechless and hurt, I just hung up and cried myself to sleep. James changed his number while he was gone. He has no intentions of coming back. I'm such a fool. Parker didn't want his dad and me seeing each other because he knew something like this would happen. Now, just as Parker predicted, everything will be awkward between the two families. With Sarah and Parker's upcoming wedding, James and I will see each other again. How will I feel if he's with a woman? I want him to be happy but it'll tear my heart out. I want to ask Parker and Sarah whether they have heard from James, but I don't. If James wants to talk to me, he has my number and my address, and he also knows where I work. He obviously doesn't want anything to do with me.

Today, like all the other days, I shower and get ready for work. I put on a fake smile and pray I'm too busy to notice the stabbing pain in the center of my heart. The shop's busy and I'm grateful for the distraction. Then I smell a familiar scent. Spice, sandalwood, and musk. My heart picks up its pace. I scan the crowded room for James but I don't see him. I'd know his cologne anywhere. Deciding it must be someone wearing the same brand of cologne of James, I attend to my next customer. That's when I see it. A white envelope with a piece of blue sea glass lying on top of it. "Grace" is written across the top in James' handwriting.

I don't touch it. "Did you see who put this here?" I ask the elderly woman in the front of the line.

"No, honey. I didn't see anything. But you sure do have a nice place here."

"Thank you. I hope you found what you were looking for," I say politely even though my mind is on the note and the sea glass.

"I sure did. Thank you."

I ring her and all the other customers up before I open the note. I prayed for a busy day and that's exactly what I got. I want to read the note, but I need to read it in private.

Finally, when the last customer leaves, I go upstairs to my apartment. I hold the sea glass tightly in my hand. Tears burn my eyes. James was here. He was in my shop yet he didn't talk to me. Is this a "Dear Grace" version of a "Dear John" letter? Why would he write me a letter instead of just talking to me?

I set the sea glass down and open the letter. My heart races as I read the small note.

Grace,

Meet me on the beach at sunset.

James

What? That's it. After a month all I get is a note that says to meet him at the beach. I look over at the fish tank and say, "Sandy Bottom Pants, is this all I'm worth?" I hold up the note as if she's going to answer me. She looks at me with fish lips and I decide she must be hungry. I feed her before deciding if I even want to meet James on the beach. Of course I do. But I would have liked to have seen him when he was in the shop.

GRACE

I prepare myself for whatever news he has to tell me. Maybe he's met a woman while vacationing in Italy. Maybe he's going to tell me being with me was a huge mistake. Maybe he's going to tell me he's gay. No, that only happens to Sarah. *Poor Sarah,* I think to myself. It might actually be less painful knowing he's with a man than it would be if he were with a woman. No, it would still be painful no matter whom he spends his time with. Maybe he's going to ask for Sandy Bottom Pants back. HELL, NO! Over my dead body. He abandoned her. She's mine now. I'd even consider taking him to court for custody. He walked out of my life and Sandy's. He'll need one hell of an argument for me to part with her.

Now I'm pissed and not so much sad about James leaving. Does Sarah know he's in town? I want more than anything to call and ask, but I don't. I'm sure he's already seen Parker. They're close.

I don't shower. I don't change my clothes or freshen my makeup. I do open a fresh bottle of wine and carry it across the street to meet him. I intentionally left later so he'd have to wait and wonder if I was even coming.

I see a small fire on the beach so I walk in that direction. My heart hurts as I remember our time on the beach with a fire. I take a big gulp from the wine bottle praying for liquid courage. As I get closer to the fire, I see a man standing at the fire with his back to me. There's a huge pile of driftwood stacked beside him. I take another big gulp as I approach him. When he hears me, he turns around. My breath catches when I see him. He's grown facial hair and his hair is longer and curlier than I remember. He's still very handsome. We just stare at each other as we take it all in. He's wearing jeans, a white hoodie, and no shoes.

"Hello, Grace," he says. He doesn't sound like his same confident self.

"James." I look around as I'm not sure what to do. There's a picnic basket sitting on top of a red and black plaid blanket. I see a small stack of firewood in addition to the stack of driftwood. There's something else that's caught my eye. There's a decorative glass jar full of sea glass next to the basket. "What's going on?" I ask.

"Would you like a glass of wine?"

I tip my own bottle to my mouth and take another big gulp. "No, I already have some." I hold the bottle out and offer it to James. Surprisingly he takes it and also takes a big gulp. "Thank you," he says, handing it back to me.

"I haven't heard from you in nearly a month. What's going on?" I ask again.

"I know and I'm sorry. Please, sit down. I have something I need to say."

I sit down careful not to kick any sand on the blanket. "Okay, I'm seated."

He sits down beside me, but he keeps a safe distance between us. "I'm sorry about how I left. I should have met up with everyone in the hotel that morning. But I left early. I had to clear my head and get everything sorted out." He pauses and I can see the sadness in his eyes. "It took me less than a day to know exactly what I wanted."

My heart feels like he just stabbed me with a dagger. If he knew what he wanted so quickly, and he never came for me, I must not be what he wanted. I look around at the picnic basket, blanket, and wine and decide this must be for someone else. This is cruel to call me over to throw it up in my face. I need to know where he went. What he's been doing.

"I see. What have you been doing these past few weeks?" I take another drink of my liquid courage. It must be working, but it's not working fast enough.

"I bought a house."

While I spent sleepless hours crying myself to sleep, he bought a house.

"That's nice. I'm happy for you." I am happy for him but that's not what I wanted to say to him. Every child on the island would need to cover their ears so they couldn't hear what I want to say to James right this instant. My face is getting hot and it's not from a hot flash or the heat from the fire. *I'm getting pissed.* "I tried to call you to see how you were doing. I was really worried about you." I decide to put my heart out there. It's already broken. He might as well stomp on it, too.

He looks shocked. "Grace, I didn't get any phone calls from you."

"You wouldn't have especially since you changed your number." I stand and take my bottle of wine with me.

"Wait a minute." He stands quickly. "What are you talking about?"

"I called you and the man who answered said this was his new cell phone number." I hold the bottle of wine tightly thankful for the courage it has given me. I continue before he can say anything. "I'm thrilled for you that you're feeling better. But do you have any idea how hurt I've been since that day?" I don't let him answer. "You promised me you'd be back. I waited for you. I worried about you. I waited for you to come back like you promised." The tears start to flow. Great! "Now you're back flaunting your new life in front of me. You've moved on and bought a new house. Well, good for you but what about me and Sandy Bottom Pants? Did we never mean anything to you? Are we that easy for you to replace?"

"Grace, you don't understand."

"No, James. I think I do. And if you think I'm giving you back Sandy Bottom Pants, you're crazy. You left her and me and she's mine now. Since we're so easily replaced, you can go out and buy yourself another fish."

I turn to storm back to my apartment. "I love you," he calls out into the night air. I stop. Did he just say he loved me? "I bought the house for us. Here on the island." His voice is getting closer. "I kept it a secret so I could surprise you. I wanted this night to be perfect so I could tell you how I feel." He stands in front of me and brushes the hair from my face. "This isn't a proposal. Not yet, anyway. Not today. But it is a promise to you. It's a promise for a brighter future for you. For me. For us. It is also a promise that I'll love you always." I lean in closer and he wraps his arms around me. I feel safe and loved. "I love you, Grace."

"Then why did you change your number?"

"I did that while Anna was calling me demanding money."

That makes sense. "Then why didn't you call me?"

"Grace. I knew you needed more than an I love you. You needed a promise for a brighter tomorrow. And I thought a house — our house — would be a start. Although I'm not ready for marriage, I am ready for a commitment. I love you, Grace."

I melt into his arms. "I love you, too."

He kisses me and I say, "How did you manage to keep it a secret? The island isn't that big, and I find it strange that we didn't run into each other."

"Let's eat and I'll tell you everything."

"That's for me?"

"Yes," he says as we walk back to the blanket.

"The driftwood?"

"It's also for you. I've been collecting it for a while now."

"The jar of sea glass?"

"For you. It's all for you. You're all I thought about. I spent every day hunting driftwood and sea glass for you, Grace."

We sit down on the blanket to eat and he tells me that he just closed on the house a few days ago. No one in the family knows about his plan to buy a house. He kept it to himself and led Parker to believe he was vacationing in Florida. He hadn't seen the house but sent Julie to look at it on his behalf since he didn't want to chance being seen by any of the family.

He admits to not knowing where or what he was going to do the morning he left the hotel, but by that evening he had it all worked out. He knew he loved me and didn't want to be without me.

"So, where's the house you bought?" The island isn't that big, and I know only a few that were on the market.

"It's a little yellow color house with a white picket fence."

My eyes get big when I think about the house he's talking about. "Does it have a small little one-room cottage in the back by the pool?"

He smiles. "It does."

"And a great view of the ocean?"

"It does."

"You bought the house next to Mom and Dad's?"

"I did."

***

It's been three months since James' nightmare ended. Three months since he gave up his home and medical practice and two months since he moved to Seashell Island full-time.

Things are moving along with James and me. It's nice having someone to do things with. Someone to have dinner with, and someone to just share my day with. He lives just a few blocks away so I see him often. We also have coffee and breakfast together along with dinner. But at night, he retires in his own space and in his own bed. Okay, not every night but some nights.

He asked me to move in with him, but I think it's too soon. Just as he needed time to sort everything out, I also need some time.

He still doesn't work but meanders around the island looking for things to do through the day. He spends some time with Parker assisting him with his practice, but I think he prefers hanging with Beau and Dad doing odd jobs for people on the island. He's replaced his suit and tie with Tee-shirts and board shorts and I have to admit, that look suits him well. He's rarely clean shaven and I love the stubble look he often wears. If I didn't know better, I'd say he was born and raised on the island. He's definitely an islander at heart.

Sarah and Parker called everyone last night to invite them to dinner tomorrow. They said they have an announcement to make. Parker has arranged a casual dinner for everyone at Jo's Tiki Hut.

"What's Sarah and Parker's big secret?" Carly asks.

"I have no idea," I say honestly.

"Really, Mom?"

"I swear. Last night she called and told me they had something to talk to everyone about, but she didn't say what it was."

"Does it have to do with James?"

"I don't think so. Why would it?"

"Because I saw Sarah and James having lunch at Jo's Tiki Hut yesterday." Now that she mentions it, I have noticed the two hanging around each other a lot lately. "Maybe this is to throw everyone off and he's going to propose to you?"

"That's not it." Is it? If James was going to propose, wouldn't I at least suspect something? He isn't acting suspiciously or any differently.

"How do you know? If I were you, I'd wear something nice just in case."

"Carly, you're always the dreamer."

"Am I?"

We hang up and now I'm beginning to wonder if she's on to something. I decide to have two outfits laid out for tonight just in case. I also decide not to get dressed until James arrives. The way he's dressed will determine what I'll wear. Sarah and Parker invited all of our family for tonight's dinner. James even asked if Julie and Tony could be there. After all, Tony is like one of the family and Julie is here visiting. It would be rude to exclude her. I'm just not sure what could be so important for everyone to be present. Tonight is about Sarah and Parker's announcement. Right? God, I hope this isn't a proposal. It's too soon. I don't want to steal the happiness from Sarah and Parker as they're still in a dilemma over their own wedding plans. Is it wrong if I pray that it isn't a wedding proposal? He wouldn't do it in a room full of people. He'd want us to be alone so we could celebrate with love making immediately after. I would also want that, too.

I decide to wear a sun dress like I had originally planned. I'm still excited to hear Sarah and Parker's announcement. Is she pregnant? Is that what they want to announce? I wouldn't care if she was. A baby? A new addition to our family would always be something to celebrate.

We eat dinner outside of Jo's Tiki Hut. The atmosphere is relaxed and laughter fills the air. Nothing is said about the reason for tonight's dinner until after dinner and just before dessert is served. By this time the chatter among everyone has died down. James squeezes my hand and says, "My son Parker and my beautiful future daughter-in-law have an announcement."

Sarah and Parker stand. I immediately look at her belly to see if she may be pregnant. The tight dress she's wearing assures me she isn't.

Parker says, "Sarah and I have finally decided on a wedding date." Everyone laughs. "I know. We've decided on many dates but this one is it. Sarah decided since her father's birthday was coming up, that his birthday would be the perfect wedding date for us. And because I'm a smart man, I agreed."

Everyone applauds and sends them congratulatory well wishes.

The excitement and happiness in the room is contagious. I know a wedding date is big news, but they're already living together and Parker already feels like family. A wedding to unite Sarah and Parker as one is definitely something to celebrate.

Later that night, James and I walk the beach and talk.

"Did you know they picked a wedding date?" I ask James.

"No, I didn't. I knew that Sarah didn't seem as stressed as she has been. I expected that the big news was from a decision that eased her anxiety level some."

I admit, "I didn't realize all the stress she had in choosing a wedding date."

"How do you feel that they decided on Michael's birthday?" he asks.

I lean into him. "I'm happy about it, but the real question is, how do you feel about it?"

"I'm fine with it. Michael was her father, and I think it's a great way to honor him.

"I also know that your marriage to him was a remarkable one. Maybe it'll be a good omen for their lifetime of happiness."

"Thank you for understanding."

"I just want you to know that when it's our time to wed, I promise to put your happiness above my own."

"James, you already do."

JAMES

I stand at the alter dressed in my best suit and wait for the bride to make her appearance. The church is full with family, friends, and islanders. Beau is standing at the podium eager to start the ceremony. I'm sure he'll be glad when Sarah and Parker are no longer living in sin.

I place a caring hand on Parker's shoulder. "Are you okay, son?"

"Never been better," he lies. "What's taking her so long? Do you think she changed her mind?"

"No." I've never been married so I have no idea what the delay is. But I do know Sarah is madly in love with my son. I look at my watch and see we still have several minutes for the ceremony to start.

Just then the music starts. We watch as Grace and her mother are ushered to the front row. It makes me feel sad that Parker's mother and Sarah's father are missing out on this special day. As a remembrance to Kara and Michael, Sarah added two tiny charms holding their photos to her bouquet. Parker asked Bea, the woman who runs the children's home to be here for him. She walks proudly as she is led to the front row of the church. She isn't Parker's mother, but she did have a hand in raising him. She played a very important role in his life and her endless search to find me. I owe her my life. Next come Sarah's grandparents and then Carly with the flower girl, Myra. It's a small wedding with only a best man and a matron of honor. I was glad when Sarah and Parker finally agreed on a wedding date. I understand it's a big time in your life, but it's just a date, so pick one already. I'm sure Sarah and every other bride on this earth would disagree with me.

Everyone stands when the bride enters the room. Sarah looks beautiful and happy. Almost as happy as Parker. The ceremony is heartfelt. The vows are read with love and true meaning. At the end when Beau announces the newly wedded couple, the room quickly quiets. At first, I thought it was a mistake.

"What did you say?" I ask, leaning up and asking Beau to repeat himself. I'm sure no one else heard him correctly either.

"I said," Beau says, clearing his throat, "Meet Mr. and Mrs. Parker Blake and family."

"And family?" I repeat softly. I look at Parker and Sarah, who are both smiling. The room erupts with cheers. She's pregnant? Quickly, I look at Grace and she's laughing and hugging her parents. Sarah turns around and hugs Carly. Parker's just looking at me and it dawns on me. "She's pregnant. With child. My son's going to be a father."

"Yes, that's right."

"You're going to be a dad, and that'll make me a grandpa."

"That's what it means."

Everyone is still clapping and hugging, and I'm trying to process everything. A huge smile spreads across my face. "My son's going to be a dad." I embrace him tightly. "Congratulations."

"Thank you. Are you sure? It looked like you were having an internal battle there for a minute."

I back away and look him in the eyes before hugging him again. My son's going to be a father. "I'm thrilled for you. I just had to process it. How far along is she?"

"She's almost three months." Which means they both knew she was pregnant the night they made the wedding date announcement. They must have just found out because Sarah didn't have a noticeable baby bump. I didn't think my son could keep a secret from me, but he sure did pull this one off.

"Are you happy, Parker?"

"I am. I have everything I ever wanted."

That's all I care about. After I hug my son, I hug my new daughter-in-law next. She's crying as she tries to keep her tears at bay. She's just one girl who has brought so much happiness into my son's life. And my life.

The reception kicks off in full gear at a local restaurant with laughter and happiness, food and drinks, friends and family. I can't remember the last time my heart felt so full. To think I may have missed out on this is beyond my comprehension. I can't imagine missing out on my son's happiness. Or my happiness on being a grandpa. I've already missed out on so much with Parker. I shift my thinking back to the present. This is what matters. Not what happened yesterday, last year, or twenty years ago.

Grace and I slow dance and fast dance. We laugh a lot and mingle with the guests. It truly is a day of celebration. To see my son this happy is something I never thought was possible. Gram and Pap are two of the first to leave. They also take Myra and Maria with them so Carly and Beau can continue with the celebration. Every chance Grace gets, she pulls me in for a photo with the professional photographer, Holly.

At the end of the night, Grace and I are among the last few to leave. We walk the beach before heading home.

Walking hand in hand she says, "Do you remember the day we saw the starfish and you told me to make a wish?"

"I do. But you wouldn't tell me what you wished for. You said it wouldn't come true."

She smiles and wraps her arms tighter around me. "I wished for this."

"A walk on the beach?" I tease.

"I wished for peace in my life, and love, and happiness, and contentment. And everything I asked for came true."

"I'm glad all of your wishes came true."

"Me, too."

"Let's sit down on the bench for a while," I say, walking on the deserted beach. "The wedding was beautiful. Sarah made a stunning bride."

"Parker was quite handsome, too. They'll make amazing parents."

"I think so."

"It feels good seeing my children so happy."

I wasn't going to do this tonight. I wasn't going to do this on Michael's birthday or on Parker and Sarah's wedding anniversary. But I bought her an engagement ring the same day I closed on the house. I was determined to win her back and if she saw the engagement ring, then maybe she would know my commitment to her was real. That my love for her was endless. She thinks tonight is perfect and nothing could make it any better. Well, I accept this as a challenge to prove to her that no matter how wonderful something is, it can always be better. Although I do have to admit a wedding is pretty hard to top.

I've been carrying the ring around with me every day since I bought it. Waiting and hoping for the perfect time to present it to her. I think this is the night.

I remove the black velvet box from my jacket pocket and kneel on one knee. Tears stream down her beautiful face before I even say anything.

"Grace, I love you. I want you to always have peace, love, happiness, and contentment in your life. I want you to always feel loved and I know I can offer all of these things to you." I open the case so she can see the ring I chose for her. "If you agree to marry me, I promise with every fiber of my being that I'll always put your happiness above my own." I remove the ring and hold it close to her left hand. "Will you please be my wife? Grace, you're my soul mate and there isn't anyone else I'd rather be with."

"I didn't think it was possible," she says through her tears. "You just made the perfect night even better."

"Is that a yes?"

"Yes, I love you, James."

I slide the ring on her finger and it's a perfect fit. "I love you, Grace." I stand and kiss her passionately. "I promise I will always love you."

The End

To continue reading more about the characters in the Seashell Island Series, watch for *Moving to Seashell Island* featuring the same characters you have grown to love and some new ones.

BOOKS BY BRENDA KENNEDY

I support Indie Authors. If you read this book, please take the time to go to the purchasing site and give it a review.

Independent authors count on your reviews to get the word out about our books. Thank you for taking the time to read my books and taking the extra time to review them. I appreciate it very much.

Books in the Seashell Island Stand-alone Series

Book One: *Home on Seashell Island*

Book Two: *Christmas on Seashell Island*

Book Three: *Living on Seashell Island*

Book Four: *Moving to Seashell Island*

Other books written by this author include:

The Starting Over Trilogy

Book One: *A New Beginning* (Free)

Book Two: *Saving Angel*

Book Three: *Destined to Love*

The Freedom Trilogy

Book One: *Shattered Dreams* (Free)

Book Two: *Broken Lives*

Book Three: *Mending Hearts*

The Fighting to Survive Trilogy

Round One: *A Life Worth Fighting* (Free)

Round Two: *Against the Odds*

Round Three: *One Last Fight*

The Rose Farm Trilogy

Book One: *Forever Country* (Free)

Book Two: *Country Life*

Book Three: *Country Love*

The Forgotten Trilogy

Book One: *Forgetting the Past* (Free)

Book Two: *Living for Today*

Book Three: *Seeking the Future*

The Learning to Live Trilogy

Book One: *Learning to Live* (Free)

Book Two: *Learning to Trust*

Book Three: *Learning to Love*

Stand-alone books in the "Another Round of Laughter Series" written by Brenda and some of her siblings: Carla Evans, Martha Farmer, Rosa Jones, and David Bruce.

Cupcakes Are Not a Diet Food (Free)

Kids Are Not Always Angels

Aging Is Not for Sissies

ACKNOWLEDGMENTS

My husband, Rex: Who would have known where this journey has taken us? Thank you for supporting me in following my dreams. Thank you for giving me the freedom to spread my wings and catching me when I fall. Thank you for always believing in me. You are my partner for life, and I love you.

My children: Thank you for reminding me what is important every single day. I love you.

My grandchildren: Thank you for reminding me that I am somebody; I am your grandma and nothing else matters. I love you all.

My sisters and brothers: Thank you for your endless support. I love you.

My brother David: Without you, I wouldn't have been able to publish the first book. Thank you for making my ideas better and for all you do. Editing, proofreading, polishing, formatting, ideas, articles, and research websites. See, I do pay attention. Thank you. Thank you for pushing me until I get it right. Maybe someday I'll learn the right place to put the commas. I love you and I can never thank you enough. David writes collections of anecdotes such as *The Funniest People in Comedy*, and he retells classics in such books as *Ben Jonson's* Bartholomew Fair: *A Retelling* and *Dante's* Divine Comedy: *A Retelling in Prose*. His books can be found for sale on all leading online electronic book sale platforms. He is apparently either the first or second person in the world to translate all 38 of William Shakespeare's plays into today's English. He may also be the first person in the world to translate at least three of Ben Jonson's plays into today's English. David wrote the all the haiku that appear in this book.

Christina Badder, I hope you know how much I appreciate your hard work and dedication. You are amazing, and I am so glad I found you.

Becki Angle Martin: Thank you for designing this stunning cover. You saw my vision and brought it to life. Thank you. I'm proud to call you family.

Thank you to all of my Beta readers: I appreciate your honest opinions and reviews, and I love the bond that we have developed. Also, I appreciate that I can trust you and count on you. Thank you for encouraging me to write and for giving me ideas. You never disappoint. I love you guys!

Thank you to "Brenda's Street Talkers" for sharing my books, making teasers and banners, and for the love and support I receive from you every day. I love you girls.

A very special thank you to author DB Jones for your endless and continuous support. I feel like I've known you my entire life.

Thank you to Delta Daun Baughman who came up with the name for James' Beta fish: Sandy Bottom Pants. I still laugh every time I say it, write it, or think about it.

To my readers: Thank you for reading and reviewing my books. Thank you to my loyal readers who have followed me from the beginning and to those who are new to me.

For those readers who enjoy a darker, more intense read: My daughter Carleen Jamison has published her debut novel, which is titled *Inappropriate Reactions*. It is Book One of the Mind Games Series. This book is intended for mature audiences only and is available on all leading online eBookstore platforms. You can follow her on her Smashwords Author's page:

https://www.smashwords.com/profile/view/carleenjamison

Info for David Bruce, My Brother

Smashwords (Books for Sale, and Free Books)

http://www.smashwords.com/profile/view/bruceb

WordPress Blog

https://davidbruceblog.wordpress.com

Download Free davidbrucehaiku PDFs Here:

https://davidbruceblog.wordpress.com/patreon/

ABOUT THE AUTHOR

Brenda Kennedy, an award-winning and bestselling author, is a true believer of romance. Her stories are based on the relationships that define our lives—compassionate, emotionally gripping, and uplifting novels with true-to-life characters that stay with her readers long after the last page is turned.

Her varied, not always pleasant, background has given her the personal experience to take her readers on an emotional, sometimes heart-wrenching, journey through her stories. Brenda has been a struggling single mom, a survivor of domestic abuse, waitress, corrections officer, hostage negotiator, and corrections nurse. She is also a wife, mom, and grandmother. Even though her life was not always rainbows and butterflies, she is a survivor and believes her struggles have made her the person she is today.

Brenda is the author of the award-winning book *Forever Country* (The Rose Farm Trilogy Book 1, for Best Book in Series). She has been dubbed "The Queen of Cliffhangers" by her adoring readers because books one and two in her trilogies almost always have a cliffhanger ending. In Brenda's own words, "I write series that end in cliffhangers, because I love them. I always give away the first book in each cliffhanger series so you have nothing to lose by reading it."

Her books have appeared on the *Publishers Weekly* Top 25 Best-Sellers list eleven times—once she had four titles on the list at the same time—along with Amazon, iBooks, and Barnes and Noble rankings in the top 100 books in contemporary romance.

Brenda moved to sunny Florida in 2006 and never looked back. She loves freshly squeezed lemonade, crushed ice, teacups, wine glasses, non-franchise restaurants, ice cream cones, boating, picnics, cookouts, throwing parties, lace, white wine, mojitos, strawberry margaritas, white linen tablecloths, fresh flowers, lace, mountains, oceans, and Pinterest. She also loves to read and write and to spend time with her family.

You may follow her on:

FB author page: http://on.fb.me/1ywRwmI

BookBub Author's Page: https://www.bookbub.com/authors/brenda-kennedy

GoodReads: http://bit.ly/1szWiw5

Twitter: https://twitter.com/BrendaKennedy_

Webpage: http://brendakennedyauthor.com

Printed in Great Britain
by Amazon